"I want you, Rafe," she said.

Her whole body quivered with nerves and desire. "I want you to hold me close."

This nightmare of Ally's could be no more than trickery, he thought with sudden anger. "I see." Rafe's voice was harsh. "We make love until dawn, then you fly off to Sydney and your brilliant career."

"How can you be so cold to me?" Ally implored, holding his hand to her breast so he could feel the chaos inside her. "I know I did something dreadful, but can't you try to understand?"

"Ally, please, no more. I've spent years killing off my feeling for you. Roll over and go back to sleep. I'm not even tempted."

"You're in as much pain as I am." How could he not be aware of the passion that had always been between them? "I want you, Rafe." Her lips parted on a shaky breath. "I need you." It came out as a quick sob. She needed to tell him how much she loved him. How she had always loved him. Always would....

Dear Reader,

Ever since I can remember, our legendary Outback has
had an almost mystical grip on me. The cattlemen have
become cultural heroes, figures of romance, excitement
and adventure. These tough, dynamic, sometimes
dangerous men carved out their destinies in this new
world of Australia as they drove deeper and deeper into
the uncompromising Wild Heart with its extremes of stark
grandeur and bleached cruelty.

The type of man I like to write about is a unique and
definable breed—rugged, masculine and full of vigor. This
Outback man is strong yet sensitive, courageous enough to
battle all the odds in order to claim the woman of his
dreams.

The Bridesmaid's Wedding is the second of three linked
books where I explore the friendships, loves, rivalries and
reconciliations between two great Australian pioneering
families. They are truly LEGENDS OF THE OUTBACK.

Margaret Way

Each story can be read independently, but together they
create an intimate family saga.

THE BRIDESMAID'S WEDDING

Margaret Way

Legends of the Outback

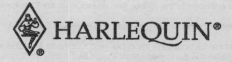

HARLEQUIN®

TORONTO • NEW YORK • LONDON
AMSTERDAM • PARIS • SYDNEY • HAMBURG
STOCKHOLM • ATHENS • TOKYO • MILAN • MADRID
PRAGUE • WARSAW • BUDAPEST • AUCKLAND

ISBN 0-373-03607-8

THE BRIDESMAID'S WEDDING

First North American Publication 2000.

Copyright © 2000 by Margaret Way, Pty, Ltd.

Visit us at www.eHarlequin.com

Printed in U.S.A.

CHAPTER ONE

BRISBANE in June. Sky meets the bay in an all-consuming blue, glorious in the sunshine. Brilliant flights of lorikeets dart in and out of the blossoming bottlebrushes, drunk on an excess of honey. Chattering parties of grey and pink galahs pick over the abundant grass seeds on the footpaths, not even bothering to fly off as someone approaches. The twenty-seven larkspur hills that surround the river city glow with wattles, the national emblem, a zillion puffballs of golden yellow flowers drenching the city in irresistible fragrance.

In the parks and gardens, the ubiquitous eucalyptus turn on an astonishing colour display as do the bauhinias, every branch quivering with masses of flowers—bridal white, pink, purple and cerise—like butterflies in motion, a foil for the pomp of the great tulip trees with their scarlet cups. All over suburbia, poinsettias dazzle the eye while the bougainvillea, never to be outdone, cover walls, fences, pergolas and balconies with sweeping arches of pink, crimson, purple, gold and bronze, but none more beautiful than the exquisite bridal white. A surpassing sight.

It was on just such a June afternoon, beloved by brides, Broderick Kinross, master of the historic cattle station Kimbara, in the giant state of Queensland's far southwest, was married to his beautiful Rebecca in the garden of the graceful Queensland colonial Rebecca's father, a retired airline captain, had bought when he and his second family returned home from his long-time base in Hong Kong. The wedding ceremony and reception were deliberately low key in accordance with the bride's and groom's wishes, with family and close friends, but a huge Outback reception was planned on Kimbara when the couple returned from their honeymoon in Venice.

Now in the rear garden bordered by the deep, wide river, some seventy guests were assembled, revelling in the sparkling sunshine and the stirring uplift of emotions. Even the breeze gave off soft tender sighs, showering blossom out of the trees like so much confetti. All faces wore smiles. Some like the bridegroom's aunt, the internationally known stage actress, Fiona Kinross, superbly dressed in yellow silk with a marvellously becoming confection on her head, registered transports of rapture. This was a wonderful day; the family wedding, the culmination of a great romance.

As the hour approached, everyone looked expectantly towards the house when quite suddenly the bride's four attendants, three bridesmaids and one little flower girl, the bride's enchanting little stepsister Christina, appeared, moving down the soaring palm-dotted lush sweep of lawn to some wondrous floating music by Handel.

Each bridesmaid was a natural beauty. Each had fabulous long hair, sable, titian and blonde, left flowing over bare shoulders, with tiny braids at the sides and back woven with seed peals, miniature silk roses in the same shade as their gowns with flashes of gold leaves. Their ankle-length sheath gowns of delustred satin showed off their willowy figures to perfection, the strapless bodices decorated with delicate pearl and crystal beading that glittered in the sunlight, the precise shades of the gowns chosen to be wonderfully complementary, rose pink, jacaranda blue, a delicate lime green.

In their hands they carried small trailing bouquets of perfect white butterfly orchids on a bed of ferns. The little flower girl dressed in lilac silk organdie with a wide satin sash, was smiling angelically, scattering rose petals from her beautifully decorated flower basket. All four of them shimmering in the radiant light, irresistible in their youth and beauty.

"Oh, the magic of being young!" Fee whispered with a catch of emotion to the tall, distinguished man standing next to her. "They might have stepped out of a painting!"

A sentiment apparently shared by the other guests who broke into cries of delight and a great wave of "Aahs."

Only one person felt strangely alone, almost isolated, but no one would have ever guessed it. Rafe Cameron, best man, with his golden leonine mane, fine features and air of authority and pride. Rafe had his own thoughts, far-ranging yet fiercely close. Thoughts that stirred an unwelcome rush of bitterness that had no part in this wonderful day. But Rafe was human. A strong man of correspondingly strong emotions who had known rejection and heartache and never got used to it.

Now he stood rooted, staring up at the ravishing tableau, his eyes drawn hypnotically towards the chief bridesmaid in her beautiful rose gown. Ally Kinross. Brod's much loved younger sister. The girl who had stolen his heart and left him with a bitter dark void in exchange. It was an agony to him how beautiful she looked, a smile of utter luminosity on her face, her magnificent curly dark hair—cosmic hair he had once labelled it in fun—hair with a life of its own, tracking down her back, the sun striking all the sparkling little gems woven into the long strands. Her perfect olive skin was pale but high colour burned in her cheeks, a sure sign of her inner excitement.

Oh, Ally, he mourned deep inside of him. Have you any idea what you did to me? But then, they never had used the same measure. Ally's protestations of undying love were like tears that quickly dried up.

Brod and Rebecca. It should have been Ally and me. He could scarcely credit it now, but this joyous occasion could have been for them. Hadn't they planned on getting married, even when they were kids? It was almost something they took for granted. The two great pioneering families, Kinross and Cameron, were surely destined one day to be united? Even Stewart Kinross, Brod's and Ally's difficult, autocratic, late father had wished it. Except it didn't happen. Ally had turned her back on him, running off to Sydney to make a name for herself as an actress just like her extraordinary aunt Fee, who now stood smiling brilliantly, looking fantastically nowhere near her age. Ally would look just like that when she was older. Both had the same marvellous bone structure to fight the years. Both had that laughing, vibrant and I-can-do-anything nature. Both knew how to take men's hearts and break them. It was in the blood.

Determinedly Rafe pushed the thought from his mind. This wasn't the day for self-pity, God knows. He rejoiced in his great friend's good fortune but he was beginning to feel his practised smile stretch on his mouth. It was this first sight of Ally that had thrown his hardwon detachment into uproar. He only hoped no one would notice, not realising how very successful he had become at masking his emotions. But hell, he was supposed to be tough. A Cameron which counted for a lot in this part of the world A Cameron respected by his peers. A Cameron brought unstuck by a Kinross woman.

And it wasn't the first time. But they were old stories. Everyone at the wedding would know them.

Rafe wrestled down the old anguish, rewarded by a moment's powerful diversion as right on cue the bride, on the arm of her proud father, appeared on the upper terrace moving from the shade of the wide verandah into the sunburst of light. She was wearing a lovely smile, posing for a time as though exquisitely conscious of her impact.

Rafe for all his hurt felt his own mood lifting, hearing Fee exclaim, "Magic!" above the great wave of spontaneous applause.

The bride remained on the terrace a short time longer so everyone could look at her, her great sparkling eyes dominating her face, her hands clasped loosely on her beautiful trailing bouquet of white roses, tulips and orchids. Like her bridesmaids she wore a slim-fitting gown, an overlay of gossamer-thin silver lace, over an ice blue satin sheath that reached to her delicate ankles and showed off her exquisite handmade shoes. She didn't wear the traditional veil. Her thick glossy hair was drawn back into the very fashionable "Asian" style, a little reminiscent of Madame Butterfly, decorated high on the crown with tiny white orchids and little cascades of seed pearls and crystals. She wore no jewellery except for the dazzling diamond studs in her earlobes, a wedding present from her adoring groom.

For the shortest time, something she couldn't possibly indulge on such a day, a kind of broken-hearted sadness swept over Fee. Memories she had learned to suppress. Her two failed marriages, all wrong really, right from the start, but she had her child, her beautiful Francesca, more precious to her with every passing day. In retrospect it seemed she had failed though she had been judged highly successful in the eyes of the world as an acclaimed actress; a countess for almost twelve years until the terrible divorce when she had been out of her mind with a short-lived passion for her then lover, an American film star more famous than she. The lunatic years, she thought of them now. Lust never becomes love. And she had had to say goodbye to her lovely little daughter who remained in the custody of her father.

"Fee, darling, you're looking very sad." Her companion bent his pewter-coloured head. "Is anything the matter?"

"Memories, Davey, that's all." Fee turned slightly to squeeze his arm. "My mind was wandering like a bird in the breeze. I'm an emotional creature at the best of times."

Lord wasn't that the truth! David Westbury, first cousin to Fee's ex-husband, Lord de Lyle, the Earl of Moray, smiled down on her wryly. The bold and bewitchingly beautiful Fee. He couldn't remember a time when he hadn't found her captivating, for all the family had never wanted de Lyle to marry her. They feared what his own ultra-conservative mother, sister to de Lyle's mother, had called her "gaudiness," her palpable sex appeal, the richness and "loudness" of her voice, which was really her training, the resonance that could reach to the back seat of a theatre, the terribly foreseeable conflict of interests. The family turned out to be right but David knew for a fact Fee had given his cousin his only glimpse of heaven for all it came with a heavy price.

"Here comes the bride," Fee began to hum, doing her best to forget her own deep regrets. "Be happy, my darlings!" she breathed.

"Amen!" David seconded beneath his breath, feeling

enormously proud of his own young relative, Francesca, the titian-haired bridesmaid in the lovely blue gown. He was so glad Fee had kept up the family ties, inviting him out to Australia for the wedding and the promise of a long luxurious holiday in the sun. Four years now since he had lost his dearest Sybilla, the *nicest* woman he had ever known. Four sad rather empty years.

Even from as far away as Australia Fee had shown her concern. "You want a bit of mothering, Davey," she had announced over the phone in that still wildly flirtatious voice. Even steeped in depression that had made him laugh. Fee had never known how to "mother" anyone, least of all her own daughter Francesca.

The focus of all eyes, Rebecca and her father began to move down the short flight of stone steps flanked by golden cymbidium orchids in great urns, smiling at the guests in front of her. It was all dreamlike in its perfection, Fee thought, her eyes stealing to the Gothic archway specially erected for the wedding ceremony. It was decorated with masses and masses of fresh flowers and beneath the arch stood her adored nephew, Brod, looking wonderfully handsome, his traditional male attendants by his side; the splendid Cameron brothers, Rafe, the best man, then Grant, the sun flaring off their golden heads. Next to Grant, a six-footer-plus like the rest of them, Brod's long-time friend and fellow polo player, Mark Farrell, all four, lean, rangy bodies resplendent in long-jacketed slate blue suits with white, pleated, front-wing collared shirts.

The bridegroom wore a royal blue Italian-style cravat, his attendants, silver. It was all dreamlike in its perfection, Fee thought. As one's wedding day should be.

Now the ceremony was due to begin. The celebrant

was waiting, moved by the atmosphere of reverence that settled over the assembly like a veil....

Throughout the marriage ritual, Rafe stood fair and square beside his friend, smoothly handing Brod the bridal ring at just the right moment, his heart deeply touched by the obvious happiness of the bride and groom. Rebecca had changed greatly from the ice-cool young woman he had first met. Secure in Brod's love she had blossomed like a closely furled bud into radiant flower, the warmth that had always been in her, quenched by a disastrous first marriage, bubbling to the surface. Nowadays Rebecca was brimming with life, a wonderful transformation with Brod beside her.

As bride and groom were pronounced man and wife, he couldn't control the pressing desire to look towards the young woman who had beguiled then betrayed him, though it showed him danger. Those *laughing* green eyes, witch's eyes, forever promising and cajoling, were glittering with tears.

Tears?

His jaw was sore from clenching it. Where was his strength? He wasn't going to share any tears with her though her glance locked with his at precisely the same moment, as though reminding him openly. It perturbed him there was so much anger left inside him, so much misery he had shoved into a dark corner. She had hurt him that badly. But she wasn't going to know about it. The tenderness towards her that had been so much a part of him at least had vanished. Ally might be a superb actress but he wasn't too bad at acting a part himself. God knows he'd had plenty of practice.

His tanned, golden face wearing a masterpiece of a smile, Rafe congratulated his friend, clamped him affectionately around the shoulders, and kissed Rebecca's satin cheek, wishing her all the happiness in the world. He told the bridesmaids, Francesca, Fee's beautiful daughter, and Caroline, Rebecca's long-time friend, they looked absolutely perfect before turning to Ally, who was unashamedly wiping the few spilt tears from her cheeks.

"It must be fantastic to marry the woman you love," he remarked as though there wasn't a single dark corner left in him. "I've never seen Brod so happy or so utterly at peace."

His voice was deep and relaxed, yet Ally winced as if from a sharp sting. Knowing him so well, she was aware of the fires that burned deep inside him, the feelings of betrayal so smoothly hidden but a hundred times worse since the last time she had seen him at her father's funeral. The message behind his words told her very clearly he would never take her back again. She wanted to go into his arms. Hug him. Beg his forgiveness, his understanding. But she knew she couldn't.

Instead she answered gently, "It was a beautiful ceremony. Perfect. I'm going to miss my big brother." Her expression turned nostalgic. "Motherless, and with the way Dad was, Brod and I were so close."

Rafe tried to deal with a stab of pity. He wanted to stretch out a hand to her. Stroke her sumptuous wild hair. Wind it around his hand like he used to. Just the slightest breeze and it ruffled into a million curls.

"You haven't lost him, Ally," he managed.

"I know." Ally felt the same old powerful tug towards him. "But Rebecca is the number one woman in his life now."

"And rightly so." Rafe's tone was crisp. "You want it that way, don't you?" He looked across the throng of guests to the radiant bride and groom happily receiving kisses and congratulations and a little bit of warm teasing.

"Of course I do!" She lifted her face to him in her spirited way. "I'm thrilled. I love Rebecca already. It's just that…"

Of course he knew. He was just trying to stir her up a little. "The family has regrouped," he relented. As a Cameron, Brod's best friend, and Ally's once-taken-for-granted future husband, he knew just how dysfunctional the Kinross family had been. The late Stewart Kinross had been a hard, complex man, barely hiding his resentment of his charismatic son, subtly making Ally suffer. Brod and Ally had had to look to one another for understanding and support all their young lives. "Brod is married now," he continued, "life goes on. But you haven't lost your brother, Ally. Just gained a sister."

"Of course." She gave her beautiful smile. "It's just that weddings are serious times, aren't they? Full of happiness, but a little sadness, too. Days when none of us seem to be able to tuck our emotions safely out of sight." She allowed herself to look into his eyes. They were so beautiful. Gold-flecked, neither grey nor green but an iridescent mix of both.

"Is that a shot at me?" he challenged.

At least they were talking, she thought gratefully. "Will we ever be friends again, Rafe?" she asked, avoiding an answer.

He chose to ignore the traitorous twist of his heart. Friends? he thought grimly. Was that what we were? He wasn't going to permit this blatant appeal to his senses, either. "Why, Ally, darling," he drawled, "I can't remember a time when we weren't."

She didn't have to touch her cheeks to know they were on fire. She supposed she deserved this. His distinctive strong-boned face with the Cameron cleft chin, looked forged in gilt. He was a splendid creature full of power and energy, beautiful really with that mane of gold hair, another Cameron hallmark. There was an enormous guardedness in his expression, yet a glimmer of something even he couldn't control, the powerful physical attraction that had once dictated their lives.

Oh, God. I need you, Ally thought. I want you. I love you. I bitterly regret running away from you and bringing about my own destruction. She realised with hidden grief the strength of her feelings far from abating over time had become more desperate. Only Rafe was a proud man like all the Camerons. A man who placed an immense value on loyalty and she had betrayed him. One of those false steps in life when she had placed self-fulfilment or how she had thought of it then, above a love so strong and deep it had all but taken possession of her. Love isn't always safe. At twenty years old the force of it had panicked her. Against everyone's wishes, she had fled. Now this. Lifelong estrangement from Rafe. It made her want to weep.

"Why look so heartbroken?" He cocked a golden brown eyebrow.

"You forget how well I know you." Though she smiled, Ally kept her telltale eyes veiled. "You're even more remote since the last time I saw you. I'm fearful you've *totally* shut me out."

"For good, darling," he assured her without apparent regret. A dark wing of her hair with its decorated little braid fell forward onto her cheek and despite himself he found he was tucking it back.

Fool! Only Ally always had been too much to handle. When he spoke it seemed imperative he make his position perfectly clear. Now his eyes were trapped by the wide beautiful shape of her mouth. The eager, ardent mouth he had kissed a thousand times. And never enough. "I've got my life together," he said by way of explanation. "I'd like to keep it that way. But don't think I'm not grateful for what we had. The bond between us will last. It's just I'm not your willing captive any more."

She gave a low sceptical laugh. "Captive? I could as easily capture an eagle. In my memory it was the other way round."

"You were always one-eyed," he said in his deep seductive voice. "Who was the girl who at age fourteen told me she adored me. That she wanted to live with me all her life. You were going to marry me the day you turned eighteen. Remember, Ally? You the born seductress. Remember how you told me you belonged to me? Remember how you drove me crazy with desire when I'd made a sacred vow I wouldn't touch you until you were old enough to handle our relationship. Poor me," he mocked, "it was my duty to protect your vulnerable innocence."

Her eyes flickered, moved away. "You were always very gallant, Rafe. A gentleman in the grand manner."

She gave a passing guest that incandescent smile that somehow flooded him with anger. "But you changed all that, didn't you?" He looked down into her face. "And maybe that was the big mistake. When it came right down to it, the fire you *thought* consumed you couldn't match the fire in me. You were the candle to the inferno, or something like that. A reckless child to the man. Is that what frightened you away?"

Because there was a hard kernel of truth in it, Ally tossed back her head, causing her long hair to bounce along her back. "You didn't find fault with me when I was in your arms,'' she retaliated, her heart swelling with emotion. She had a vivid flash of the way it was, an experience so momentous, like nothing else that had ever happened to her, their bodies bonding passionately in the great front bedroom at Opal. A bedroom not slept in since Sarah and Douglas Cameron, Rafe's and Grant's parents, had been killed in a light aircraft crash returning home to the station. But Rafe had wanted it that way. Wanted their first mating in the immense ancestral bed. A night without sleep. Delirious making love.

Rafe. Her first love. Only love. There had been other relationships since, a very few; the ones she had settled for a second best, none with that tremendous *significance*. None who could make her soar. Mind, body, spirit. No one. Rafe was her past, her present. Life without him in the future was unimaginable. He was the missing piece of the jigsaw of her life without which the whole design could never be resolved.

She should have married Rafe years ago when she'd had the chance, instead of fleeing his powerful aura. Rafe, like her brother Brod, had inherited wealth, power, responsibility. A life of service to the land. She understood it, bred to the same heritage, but she couldn't pretend she had the same dedication. Now years later she would give that dedication gladly. Her career had brought her public admiration, the respect of her peers, but it hadn't brought her either happiness or fulfilment. It had brought her a good deal of hard work, terrible hours, and increasingly a level of anxiety she had never remotely anticipated. There was a high price to pay for fame.

"Ah, well, it's all in the past," Rafe was saying gently without sounding remotely friendly. "I propose we leave it there instead of raking over the dying embers. You know that. So do I. Although it seems a pity your great career isn't as fulfilling as you thought?''

With an abrupt movement she took a little step back from him, raising her chin. ''Who told you that?''

He wagged a finger at her. ''Ally, Ally, because I can match you step for step, beat for beat, word for word. I know you as well as you know me. You're not happy in your make-believe world. You used to say you couldn't breathe in the city. *And* because I liked you the way you were,'' his gaze moved down over her, deceptively silky, ''I have to tell you you're way too thin.''

''Great! I look awful?'' she mocked. She knew without vanity how good she looked even if stress was taking its toll.

He considered the question briefly, golden head, metallic in the sunlight, to one side. ''Well, put it this way. You're not quite as much woman as you used to be. There's not an awful lot on top.'' He glanced meaningfully at her fitted strapless bodice. ''But you look beautiful. The sort of woman one can't take one's eyes off. Totally desirable. Which makes me wonder why there's never any affair of yours splashed over the cover of the women's magazines?''

''Somehow I still believe my private life is my own. Anyway, since when have women's magazines appealed to you?'' She spoke sweetly, aware as Rafe must be, they were the focus of many eyes. A splendid affair gone wrong like Scarlett and Rhett.

''Ever heard of women friends?'' His dry tone glittered. ''I was over at Victoria Springs only the other day, submerging myself in old issues with Lainie. The two of us went through them together. Lainie has always been one of your greatest admirers. Four pages of Ally Kinross wears seductive separates, that was in *Vogue*.

Mercifully you put them *together*. I figured you could have worn a bra with the see-through number, Lainie predictably thought you looked fabulous. There was Ally Kinross acting up a storm; Ally Kinross tells us about her working life. No wonder you've lost weight, but no mention of your love life, though. I say that's odd. Neither of us is getting any younger.''

Which was true. ''Perhaps you'll show me the way,'' she retorted with a spark of anger. ''You and Lainie share the same tastes. Very establishment, very conventional and so forth.'' Was she so jealous? Of Lainie, their friend?

He made a soft, jeering sound. ''To hell with that! You're talking nonsense.''

''Am I? It seemed to me the relationship has flourished,'' she commented, believing it to be true, ''so don't look down your ridiculously straight nose at me. Though at five-seven, allow a couple more inches for heels, not a lot of people do. But *you* can.'' Rafe, like her brother Brod, stood an impressive six foot three.

''I expect being a tall woman has its problems?'' he said, a lazy smile to his so sexy mouth.

''You found your way around them.'' Despite herself she sparked again. ''You've changed, Rafe. You never used to be sarcastic.''

''Forgive me. I'm so sorry.'' He seemed to find that amusing. ''Anyway, that's the least of your problems.'' He saluted a passing guest who didn't make the mistake of butting in. Rafe's and Ally's unique relationship was known to all of them.

''I didn't say I had any problems,'' Ally began to realise she and Rafe had stood a little too long talking. Everyone was moving off to the huge white marquee erected in the grounds, among the guests an attractive young woman in an exceptionally pretty flower-printed chiffon dress with a sparkling ornament securing her cascade of long, thick, fair hair. Lainie Rhodes from Victoria Springs Station. Lainie, although a couple of years younger than Ally, had been part of everything from childhood. "So you're not admitting you've turned up the heat on your friendship with Lainie?" Lainie wished it was otherwise but she couldn't control her need to know. Her eyes followed Lainie's high-spirited progress, arm in arm with Mark Farrell, the groomsman.

"It sounds like you don't care for that?" Rafe countered very dryly, trying to blanket out his own warring emotions. Lainie was a nice girl. He was fond of her, but he hadn't gotten around to seeing her as more than "the girl next door."

Yet. The hard fact was he had a responsibility to get married. Produce an heir for Opal. It was imperative he find a solution to Ally. A good woman to combat her.

Knowing him so intimately Ally picked up on his wavelength. "Lainie is one of us," she said almost in quiet resignation. "We used to compete in the show ring. She's fun and very loyal."

"Totally different from you." It was cruel. A bitter accusation he couldn't prevent from rushing out.

Cut to the heart, Ally, the accomplished actress, turned her response into provocative banter. "You mean, I don't remind you of a friendly puppy?"

But Rafe, too, had recovered his equilibrium. "I meant that in the nicest way possibly." He wasn't at all fazed by Ally's reminding him of a chance remark he had once made about Lainie. There was a time she had practically leapt into his lap every time she saw him, which was the way her teenage crush seemed to take her.

"Obviously." Ally nodded in agreement. "May we expect an announcement?" Though she continued to speak breezily it was taking all her training. She felt she couldn't bear an answer that suggested a growing involvement.

"Ally, darling, let me set you straight." Rafe reverted to a sardonic drawl. "My private life no longer has a great deal to do with you. No offence. Just a simple statement of fact. What we had I'll remember all my life, but it's *over*. Something that happened at another time. To different people. Ah, here's Grant and Francesca coming our way," he exclaimed like a man granted a reprieve. "I'm sure you've noticed they get on amazingly well, though don't read anything into that. The Lady Francesca has her own brilliant life in London."

"She might like to change it." Ally, too, watched her cousin Francesca and Rafe's brother Grant walking arm in arm towards them. Francesca of the glorious titian hair looked ravishingly pretty in her jacaranda blue bridesmaid's dress, not even reaching to Grant's broad shoulder. Grant, like Rafe, was outrageously handsome. He and Fran looked wonderful together, their laughter spinning out to reach them. Happy, carefree laughter. The sort of laughter one wants to hear at a wedding. Ally was enormously fond of her cousin, Lady Francesca de Lyle. The idea of having Francesca around all the time had immense appeal.

Not apparently to Rafe.

"Don't say that!" he murmured, half amused, half alarmed. "I don't want to see my brother's heart broken, as well."

Her breath seemed to leave her. *As well?* "Are you admitting you still have some feeling left for me?" She held his eyes, eyes that had once been infinitely loving. Eyes that still had such power over her.

"I'm saying I *did,* until you got bored and ran away." His marvellous body relaxed. "Sometimes it seems a pity your spell lost its potency, Ally. I might never feel that kind of heat again. Ah, the feverishness of youth!" His voice was light with nostalgia. "Such a dangerous time."

"At least it gave you a good excuse to hate me."

"Hate you?" He stared at her in mock shock. "I can't get stuck with that one, Ally. I'd never dream of hating you. What do they say about one's first love? Never mind." He extended a courteous arm to her. "Why don't we join up with brother Grant and your Francesca? Most people have made their way to the marquee. I want to see all the delectable things to eat. I let lunch go so I'd have plenty of space. I just love weddings. Don't you?"

CHAPTER TWO

THE reception had been arranged as a buffet with long tables, covered in white linen cloths that had been given a deep lace edging, laden with delicious food: glazed ham and turkeys, great platters of bay oysters on beds of crushed ice, luscious seafood of all kinds—crab, prawns, lobsters, crayfish, scallops, silver trays of whole smoked salmon and capers ringed by the old favourite, quartered boiled eggs. There were fish dishes done in mouth-watering pastry, succulent slices of roast beef and lamb, pasta dishes, chicken dishes, mountains of piping hot rice and a variety of garden salads to refresh the palate. But the greatest fanfare was the dessert table. Guests stood looking at it transfixed. Some of the younger ones even started to applaud.

There were cheesecakes, shortcakes, splendid gateaux, tortes, mousses, trifles, the much loved meringues, their snowy peaks running passion fruit, or for the more so-phisticated the meringues were filled with hazelnut cream and drizzled with chocolate, the delectable whole dominated by a four-foot-high fruit and chocolate brandy wedding cake, like some wondrous sculpture. The Corinthian pillars were perfect in every detail as were the garlands of handmade flowers and lace work. As the guests continued to exclaim at the ravishing effect of decor and food, waiters in black trousers and short white jackets began to circulate, offering the finest champagne.

The moving ceremony over, the festivities began.

The idea was for the guests, all known to one another,

23

to mingle freely, moving from table to table as the mood took them, the whole atmosphere wonderfully relaxed. Only the bridal party had defined seating at the top table.

Stage one was the feasting that everyone enjoyed tremendously, then came the speeches. The next stage was the dancing, balloon and glitter-throwing. Someone even threw two or three plates before they were reminded it wasn't actually a Greek wedding.

Later on, after the bride and groom had left for their flight to Sydney where they would spend a night in a luxurious hotel before embarking on the first leg of their trip to Europe, the rest of the bridal party and some of the younger guests were going on to the theatre with supper after if anyone possibly had room for it, and there was talk of continuing on to Infinity, the "in" nightclub. No one wanted such a glorious day to end.

When it was time for the bride to change into her going-away clothes, Ally went up to her room to help her.

"This has been the most wonderful day of my life!" Rebecca announced, smiling emotionally through her tears. "Brod to share my life. I adore him. You've been wonderful to me, too, Ally. I'm so grateful for your friendship and support. You played a big part in bringing us back together. You're such a generous spirit."

"As I should be." Ally took charge of Rebecca's beautiful wedding gown. "I've taken over the role of sister."

"That's true!" Rebecca laughed shakily, stepping into the skirt of her fuchsia bouclé wool going-away suit. "I know you're going to be the best sister I could have."

It sounded so heartfelt, so full of gratitude, Ally stopped smiling. She went forward to kiss Rebecca's cheek. "Thank you for that, Rebecca," she said gravely.

"Thank you for becoming part of my family. You're going to change Brod's life in the most wonderful way. Give him such love. Family. That's what he needs."

"And you, Ally?" Rebecca looked at her new sister-in-law with her great shining eyes. "You must be happy, as well."

"I'm going to try, love." Ally was amazed her voice was so steady. "But I don't think Rafe is ever going to change his mind about me."

"You still love him." It wasn't a question but a sad statement of fact. There were no secrets between the two young women. They'd shared many a heart-to-heart discussion.

"I'll always love him." Ally went to the wardrobe to hang up Rebecca's dress. "That's just the way it is. I'll continue to love him even if he marries someone else." She closed her eyes in involuntary pain.

"You don't think your friend, Elaine...?" Rebecca asked tentatively. She couldn't help noticing Rafe had danced with Lainie Rhodes a number of times, Lainie staring adoringly into his eyes.

"Anything's possible, Becky," Ally was forced to admit. "Lainie's really nice. Warm and kind. Not a major brain perhaps but competent. She'll develop beautifully, too. She's a country woman above anything else. She knows how to continue a tradition."

"And you don't?" Rebecca turned to scrutinise her new sister-in-law, loyalty in her eyes.

"I think Rafe has convinced himself I'm another Fee," Ally explained sadly. "God knows I love Fee. We all do. It's hard not to. But Fee always took care of herself and her career above every other concern. Fran must have been a very sad and lonely little girl, for all her father tried to make it up to her. I suspect her life now isn't as glamorous as it's supposed to be, any more than mine. To love and be loved is a woman's greatest joy. Children her greatest achievement. And my biological clock is ticking away.''

"And mine.'' Rebecca sounded as though she had just the right plan to stop it in its tracks. "I had to avoid falling pregnant with my previous husband Martyn, our life being what it was, but Brod is my dream come true.'' She picked up a silk cushion and hugged it. "I feel today my life begins with him. My *real* life with me functioning the way I am, not keeping everything locked up inside. My love for Brod has invaded every aspect of my life. Loving has taken away the pain.''

"I can understand that.'' Ally nodded. "You've been wonderful for him, too. Brod and I have also had our bad times. Now,'' Ally paused, seeking to lighten the conversation, "what are you going to do with your hair?'' Rebecca had removed all the ornaments.

"I'd thought I'd leave it long,'' Rebecca picked up a brush, whisking it vigorously through her waterfall of hair. "Brod likes it this way.'' Finally she turned. "What do you think?''

"Beautiful,'' Ally smiled, handing Rebecca her fuchsia jacket.

'I mustn't forget my bouquet.'' Rebecca looked back at the exquisite arrangement lying on top of a small circular table. "I want my chief bridesmaid to catch it.''

And so Ally did, though Lainie was powerfully disappointed. She, who had manipulated herself into a good catching position, saw the bouquet sailing right for her, but somehow at the very last minute, never mind how, misjudged her timing. The bouquet cleared her outstretched hands though she was sure she stood on someone's toe to get it and landed against Ally's flawless, infinitely sexy, breast.

The irrepressible Aunt Fee, who was too much, Lainie and her mother had always thought, burst out clapping in a kind of triumph. "Isn't that great?" she demanded of the tall silver-haired man, exuding Englishness, who had certainly never left her side the entire afternoon. "You know what that means, Ally, don't you? You're next."

"Don't forget me, Mamma," Francesca laughed, holding up a single white orchid that had separated itself from all the rest. She felt wonderfully happy and alive anticipating the long evening with Grant beside her. He was so completely different from anyone she knew at home. So strong, so straightforward, so self-reliant, full of his hopes and plans. She couldn't seem to get enough of his company.

"Congratulations, darling," Rafe murmured in Ally's right ear. He was smiling sardonically, showing his perfect white teeth. "Possibly it's to someone you haven't yet met."

"Oh, that makes me so cross!" Lainie interrupted, turning round to them. "It's not as though you even tried, Ally, when I pray for a good husband every day of my life. No joke, Rafe," she cautioned him, "so stop laughing."

"Sorry, pet," he answered lazily. "Catching things was never your strong point but Ally here, was raised as a tomboy. She has an excellent eye."

"She's so amazingly beautiful she doesn't need to catch any bridal bouquet," Lainie half grumbled, looking up at him with intense helpless delight. Rafe was always charming and agreeable to her but she could scarcely believe someone like Rafe Cameron, so eligible in every way, could ever find her sexually attractive. Not after Ally who was like a bright flame, but—well everyone in the Outback knew their story. The reason for the split up. Ally, like her fabulous, over-the-top aunt, had wanted to become an actress. Simply dumping one of the most gorgeous men who had ever lived.

"How could she do such a thing?" Lainie's mother had often asked, shocked. "I don't suppose I should say it, but bolting seems to run in the family."

Now Ally was a star who won gold Logies for best actress. Lainie loved her show and tried never to miss an episode. Ally was the sort of person, who could easily make the big-time like Cate Blanchett and take on the world. She was lost to Rafe and he had to accept that. Besides, Rafe had started to spend much more time over at Victoria Springs.

"Don't be modest, Lainie," her mother had encouraged her. "You'll make any man a wonderful wife."

Possibly, but she only wanted Rafe.

So Lainie hoped and prayed and didn't enter into any other relationship. The worst part, she truly loved both of them. Ally and Rafe. She would have to have a talk with Ally as soon as she possibly could. Find out the lay of the land.

Tumultuous cheering broke out as Rebecca and Brod climbed into the limousine that was to take them to the airport. Everybody began to wave. Ally, hair flying, holding the little flower girl's hand, ran once more to the car and leant in to land yet another kiss on bride and groom. "Take care, you two. Have a wonderful time! I'll be expecting to hear from you," Ally said.

Rebecca smiled at her and her small stepsister. "Darling little Christina! I'll miss you. I'll miss you both so much."

"With me by your side?" Brod, looking unbelievably handsome in a well cut grey suit, laughed at his bride.

"You know what I mean, darling." She leaned to kiss him, a kiss that tasted of champagne and strawberries.

"It's a good thing I do." Brod's eyes left his bride's beautiful face for a moment. "Take care, Ally. You'll be hearing from us often. I've asked Rafe to keep an eye on Kimbara. *When* he can find the time. Ted's a good man but it makes me happy knowing Rafe is on hand. I'm grateful to him for so many things."

"So you should be!" Rafe, overhearing, called with affection. "Have the best time in the world, you two. Now take it away." He signalled to the chauffeur as the bridal party threw more confetti. Fee wiped it laughingly from her own and David Westbury's clothes then grasped the little flower girl's hand while Rafe got an arm around Ally's narrow waist drawing her backwards so he could shut the limousine door.

Heat like an electric charge, rushed up his arm as it came in contact with her body. Heat to his heart, to his head, to his loins. For a moment he almost despised himself with his reaction. This was like a haunting. There had to be some way to exorcise Ally. He let go of her before his whole body dissolved.

They all watched until the limousine was lost to sight then everyone began to walk back to the house, those that weren't going on to the theatre starting to say their goodbyes although Rebecca's father assured them they were welcome to stay as long as they liked, an offer a lot took up.

Lainie waited until the powder room cleared before she decided to conduct her own little investigation. She had to find out for sure if Ally still carried a torch for Rafe. She knew in her heart she would find it hard to come between them if they still cared for one another. Though one didn't hear too much about grand passions any more, thank the Lord. She could talk to Ally. Woman to woman. They went back a long way. Big TV star or not, a member of one of the great pastoral families. Well, a patrician in this part of the world, Ally was very down-to-earth and friendly.

"You look wonderful, Ally. Superb," Lainie said for starters, her large, soft, brown eyes admiring as she watched Ally make a few minor repairs to her make-up. Gosh, how did she get her eyeshadow like that? It made her slanting green eyes look like emeralds.

"Thanks, Lainie." Ally gave her lovely smile. "It's been such a beautiful day. A day I'll remember with great joy. A little sadness, too." She began to remove the decorations from a braid. They'd be too much for the theatre. Fran had removed hers, twisting her beautiful hair into a very elegant knot. Maybe she could do the same even if she couldn't get the same result. Fran's hair was wonderfully manageable, hers was downright difficult. Ally experimented for a moment until she became aware of Lainie's expression. "For heaven's sake, Lainie, why are you staring at me like that?" she asked wryly. "Has my mascara run?"

When it actually came to it, Lainie's mouth went dry. "Sorry, pal. I apologise. I was staring, I know. You must be used to it, anyway. You're gorgeous."

"You're not too bad, either," Ally reminded her. "That dress looks wonderful on you."

"I haven't been able to eat to get into it," Lainie freely admitted. "Ally, I just wanted to ask you something personal—I'd never ask if I didn't think...I mean I'd never..."

"You want to know if Rafe and I still mean something to each other?" Ally had a shot at it.

"Right on," Lainie sighed in relief. "Please don't tell me if you don't want to. I'm not a person who is ever going to be called confrontational."

"Fairly forthright nevertheless, my girl." Ally felt she no longer had the energy to fool around with her hair. She would have to leave it as it was. "Lainie, love," she explained patiently, "you know as well as anyone Rafe and I are an old story."

"But you were wonderful together." Perversely Lainie mourned. "Mum thought you had to be nuts."

"Unfortunately I was." Ally looked her regret. "But that was years ago. I was younger than you are now. I thought I needed more time before I could face so much responsibility. Rafe was master of all he surveyed. We all know what the Camerons are like. I wanted to find myself, show the world what *I* could do."

"Oh, I know, Ally." Lainie was understanding. "You wanted to be like your aunty. She was *very* famous though you don't hear much of her these days. But those challenges lost you Rafe."

"You don't have to sound pleased about it," Ally said reproachfully.

"Oh, I'm not pleased." Lainie's reply was genuine and hasty. "I feel sad. Like everyone else did. We thought we were guaranteed a huge wedding on Kimbara. You might even have chosen me for a bridesmaid."

That really shook Ally. It could have been a possibility. Now she was looking on Lainie as a possible successor.

"Are you still in love with him?" Lainie wanted everything made clear to her.

"What do you want me to say?" Ally held out a hand for Lainie to get up. It was time to go. "Rafe will always have a place in my heart. The Camerons and the Kinrosses are almost kin. We grew up together. But things happen. Rafe and I have changed. We're different people now. I have my career. It's no secret I've had movie offers."

Ally stayed a hand as Lainie's pretty mouth framed "What?" "Rafe is wedded to Opal Downs. Like Brod, his inheritance is his life. We've moved on as people."

Lainie's cheeks flushed as wild relief swept her. She clasped Ally's hand tightly. "So you don't mind if...?"

"You have my blessing, Lainie." Ally freed herself gently from Lainie's surprisingly strong grip. "But I should add some sisterly advice. I don't want to see you hurt, either. Rafe has any number of women clamouring for his attention. At least four of them are probably waiting patiently for us outside the door."

"But he was having a ball with *me*," Lainie argued.

"That's what one does at a wedding, Lainie," Ally warned her. "Have a ball."

Lainie considered that for a time. "*You're* the only one who worried me," she said finally. "Mum woke me up to the fact Rafe might consider me for a girlfriend."

"So good luck, then," Ally answered feeling she had done her best. Having a ball at a wedding didn't add up to a romance. Or did it?

The theatre show was as brilliantly entertaining as the reviews had promised. Everyone came out of the theatre feeling a flood of warmth, smiling, humming snatches of the catchy tunes.

"You're coming on with us to the nightclub, aren't

you, Ally?'' Francesca asked as they stood amid the swirling crowd in the foyer.

Ally was long used to all the glances of recognition that came her way. In another minute someone would come up and ask for an autograph. Meanwhile she smiled at her cousin, anxious now to be off. She certainly didn't want to see any more of Rafe with Lainie in tow. "I have to fly back to Sydney in the morning, Fran,'' she explained. "I have a pretty hectic schedule next week.''

"What a pity. I'd have loved you to come.'' Francesca couldn't hide her disappointment even as she understood.

"So how are you getting home?'' Grant, who was holding Francesca's slender arm, turned his tawny head to see if he could catch sight of his brother. "Rafe is somewhere back there. Maybe he could give you a lift?''

"No, that's okay.'' Ally smiled back. She realised Grant, like her own brother, Brod, had never given up hope she and Rafe would some day be reunited. "I can catch a cab.''

"You can share ours.'' Francesca didn't like the idea of Ally's going home on her own.

"You're going the other way, love,'' Ally reminded her.

"That doesn't matter.'' Francesca looked up to Grant for confirmation.

"Of course not.'' He was more than happy to oblige. "We can drop Ally off then come back into town. Where is it, Ally? Some friend lent you their unit, didn't they?''

Ally nodded. "Pam is holidaying on the Barrier Reef for a week. It seemed nicer than staying at a hotel. I like to be a bit anonymous.'' Keep my whereabouts a secret, she thought a little grimly.

"Ah, there's Rafe now. Rafe?'' Grant called to his brother who was clearly enjoying something Lainie was saying to him.

"Be with you.'' Rafe lifted a long arm, turning to shake the hand of a male guest who was moving off.

"I'm sorry, but I don't think it's a good idea if Lainie falls in love with Rafe,'' Grant announced out of the blue.

"You think she might?'' Fran looked like she'd never considered it for a minute.

"I'm sure she already has,'' Ally confirmed, turning to a youngster who came up with a program to be autographed.

"Gee, thanks, Ally, that's cool!'' The boy, who had to be all of fourteen, whistled behind his braces.

"Does he know you?'' Grant looked after the departing fan.

"No. He just thinks he does.'' Ally smiled. "I've had complete strangers come up and start talking as though they'd known me all my life.''

"I don't think I could get used to it,'' Grant said with a slight frown. "Anyway, to get back to Lainie. Rafe isn't flirting with her, he's only being nice.''

"Well he's got her up in the sky somewhere. Floating on cloud nine,'' Ally offered wryly. "Mind you, Lainie is sweet. She's entitled to her dreams.''

Grant wrinkled his broad forehead. "Just between you and me. Rafe needs a great deal more than Lainie can offer.'' He laughed shortly, the tiniest spark of anger in his hazel eyes. "Do you honestly think she's woman enough for him?'' He held Ally's gaze in his direct manner.

"Don't ask me—it's too close to home."

Francesca stared from one to the other, looking thoroughly intrigued. "Are you suggesting someone should tell poor Lainie to back off, Grant, dear?"

"It might save her a lot of heartache." Grant looked serious. "No one wants Lainie to get hurt."

Lainie, smiling brilliantly, was starting towards them and Ally began to brace herself for what was to come.

"I'm trying to talk Rafe into joining us at the nightclub," Lainie announced. "You have to help me." She appealed to Ally and Fran.

"Rafe's really not one for nightclubs, Lainie," Grant tried to warn her.

"But on such a *night*." Lainie clutched at Francesca's arm in her enthusiastic fashion. "Quite a few of us are going on. There's absolutely no need for him to rush off."

"Well, *I* have to," Ally told her lightly. "We start shooting very early Monday morning."

"I'd love to get a bit part in one of your shows," Lainie confessed. "But I suppose I'm too short."

That struck Grant as utterly irrelevant and he said so.

"It was just a thought." A little warily Lainie eyed Rafe's younger brother, knowing Grant Cameron wasn't as sweetly tolerant as Rafe was. Grant was one of those men who didn't suffer fools gladly.

Into the group came the rangy, elegant Rafe, looking super relaxed. The overhead lighting gilded his fine features and played around the smile on his sexy curving mouth. "So is everyone off?"

"You're coming, then?" Lainie rejoiced, all but rubbing her cheek against his slate blue jacket. "It's wonderful to know I could persuade you."

"Well..." Rafe looked down a moment at her fair

head. "Lainie, I find it hard to disappoint you, but I'm flying off home in the morning. Grant is staying on to line up some more business, but I have to get back to the station. As well, I promised Brod I'd keep an eye on Kimbara. You've got a dozen people to keep you company," he consoled her. "Fran and Grant are going on. So is Mark Farrell. I thought you two got on rather well." He referred to the groomsman. "And Ally must do this sort of thing all the time."

"You obviously haven't heard about my killing schedule," Ally said in a wry voice. "I have to get lots of beauty sleep so I can get up the next morning without telltale bags under my eyes."

"Bags? Not you," Lainie retorted.

"So can I drop you off at your hotel?" Rafe looked on sardonically. "You're staying with Fee and Francesca?"

"Not this time." Ally shook her head. "Fee has commandeered the best suite. Davey has another."

"I have to settle for deluxe," Francesca smiled.

"And a friend has lent me her place while she's away," Ally added.

"Rafe are you *sure* you won't come?" Lainie persisted, desperately wanting it to happen.

"Sorry, pet." He gave her his maddening nonchalant smile.

"Well, that takes care of that then," Grant said with satisfaction. "We were going to drop Ally off, Rafe, but I'm sure she's happy for you to take over."

"I don't *have* to go," Lainie looked about vaguely, wishing secretly Rafe would simply take her off to bed.

"Sure you do!" Grant took hold of her arm purpose-

fully, with Francesca, blue eyes twinkling, taking the
other. "Let the good times roll."

Grant looked back at his brother and Ally and tilted
a tawny eyebrow.

CHAPTER THREE

THEY were quiet in the taxi, each sitting as far away from each other as possible, but feeling the effects of their enforced intimacy coming at them in electric waves.

"Are you coming in for a moment?" Ally asked when they arrived. "You can have a nightcap. You don't need to drive."

He wanted to tell her no. He had already begun to shake his head, but Ally threw open the door, peering up at the apartment block. She didn't want him to see her nervousness. She didn't want him to know the cause of it. She moved towards the well-lit entrance, assuming Rafe was paying off the driver.

"Nice place," the driver said to Rafe. "Beautiful woman. I'm sure I know her from someplace. Your wife?"

"She shied away from accepting me," Rafe found himself admitting.

"Fancy that!" The driver, of Italian descent, looked amazed. This guy looked like he had it all. "I haven't seen such a glamorous couple in a long time."

The lift was empty, the hallway a blaze of illumination. They were quiet again until they reached the door of the unit.

"You know, Ally, you're nervous," Rafe observed calmly, taking the key off her and fitting it in the lock. "Not of me, surely?"

The fact was she was excited but edgy, as well. These

last months had taken their toll on her. She was starting to act like someone with a real problem, which, in fact, she had. But who could hurt her with Rafe around. He was very much the man in control.

"I could do with a cup of coffee," she admitted, giving a husky laugh.

He unlocked the door and held it open so she could precede him into the apartment. She'd left a few lamps burning as she always seemed to do these days. Now in the low rosy light she glanced automatically towards the sliding doors that led out onto the terrace with its spectacular views of the cityscape.

Something moved. She stood perfectly still, muscles tensing, adrenalin pumping into her blood.

"What is it? What's the matter?" Rafe registered her alarm instantly, grasping her arm and staring into her stricken face. "Ally?" She looked primed for panic as though her emerald eyes saw some great wrath. "What the hell's going on here?"

At the sound of his voice relief flooded into Ally's face. She could diagnose her own delusion born of months of harassment. She turned to him, her heart still racing, grateful beyond words for how he filled the room with his commanding presence.

"Rafe!" It was little more than a gasp as she waited for the adrenalin in her blood to dissipate.

"For God's sake! What did you think you saw?" he burst out, letting go of her, moving with a lithe, purposeful tread to the sliding-glass doors. Obviously she thought someone or something was out here. He saw only the night-time dazzle of the city lights and glittering towers, the graceful sweep of the Expressway spanning the broad deep river that meandered through the centre of the city in grand curves.

He turned back to her, shaking his head. "There's nothing here. Nothing to be afraid of."

"Good." She gave a small delicate sigh.

Perturbed himself now, Rafe unlocked the doors, slid them open and walked out onto the terrace. Nothing disturbed the peace. There was a collection of potted plants, a white wrought-iron table with two chairs. Quietly alert he walked to the balcony. Looked over. Directly below him five floors down a young couple was entering the building. They were laughing, hand in hand, eyes only for one another.

Ally watched him come inside, feeling slightly ashamed now of her instinctive reaction. The moment of panic. "Just a trick of the lighting," she offered by way of explanation. "I thought I saw something move."

"Something or someone?" His arresting face framed by that burning gold hair was etched with hard concern. Obviously she wasn't telling him the whole story but he intended to get it out of her. He could see she still looked scared when the Ally he knew was the least nervous of women. She had never jumped at shadows. It made him angry suddenly that life in the city should have made her so. He recognised what he felt was possessiveness. Possessiveness permeated with a sense of powerlessness. She wasn't his Ally any more.

"It was nothing, Rafe." Ally tried to shrug the moment off. "Stop looking like you want to pummel someone. I have an overactive imagination." She turned quickly towards the galley kitchen. "I'm having coffee, would you prefer Scotch?"

"Coffee will be fine." He began to roam around the open-plan entrance, living/dining room, furnished quietly but comfortably with one stunning piece of art dominating. "This must be like living in a birdcage," he muttered, a big man in a small, confined space.

"Not everyone can afford grand houses," Ally pointed out, "and vast open spaces. Actually this is quite an expensive piece of real estate."

"I imagine it would be with that view." He glanced back at the sparkling multicoloured lights reflected in the indigo river, then walked nearer the kitchen looking over the counter to where Ally was measuring coffee into a plunger. "Your hand is shaking." How beautiful her fingers were, long and elegant, the nails gleaming with a polish that matched her gown. Ringless. He still had the engagement ring he had planned to give her.

"So it is," she agreed wryly. She wanted to tell him everything. How awful it had been for her. But he might see it as a deliberate play for his sympathy.

"Why, exactly," he persisted, his lean powerful body tensing as it might against a threat.

"It's been that sort of a day."

"Something is really bothering you." He watched her closely, all his old protective feelings coming into play.

"Lord, Rafe, I'm just a little tired. And overexcited. Sit down and I'll bring the coffee over."

"It might make sense to tell me," he remarked, his face reflecting his concern. "Do you mind if I have a quick look through the place?"

"Be my guest," she answered a little weakly. Her heart was still quaking. "Two bedrooms, one used as a study, two bathrooms, a laundry."

"My God!" He sounded amazed anyone could live like that. The cattle baron with his million wild acres.

Rafe walked down the narrow corridor checking each room in turn. He even looked inside the built-in wardrobes, accepting now some terror large or small was preying on her mind.

"Well?" She arched a brow. So hard to believe he was here. So wondrous. So real.

"Everything in order." He crossed to one of the couches upholstered in some light green fabric and removed a few of the overabundant cushions. "I bet this is nothing like where you live in Sydney?" Ally had tremendous flair. They had spent a lot of time walking round the homestead on Opal planning what they would do to refurbish it after they were married. Opal Downs boasted a marvellous old homestead like Kimbara, but whereas Kimbara homestead had been constantly refurbished and updated, Opal had been caught in a time warp. Nothing much had been changed since his grandfather's time. His mother had been contemplating a lot of changes in the months before she and his father along with six other passengers, had been killed when the light aircraft they had been travelling in crashed into a hillside in the New Guinea highlands.

He couldn't bear to remember that terrible time. The shock and the grief. The last time he and Grant had seen their parents alive they had been laughing and full of life, waving from the charter plane that had taken them away from Opal. Forever.

"I've decorated my apartment. We all do our own things. You've gone very quiet." Ally, as sensitive to him as he was to her, set the tray down on the coffee table.

"Memories. They come on you without warning."

"Yes, they're the very devil!" Ally agreed, remembering all the times she had to push her own back. "I'm glad we can have this quiet time together, Rafe."

She was a siren seducing him into her arms. He could

smell the perfume that clung to her, stirring his blood. He had lived almost like a monk for years. The odd go-nowhere affair. But there was a huge difference between having sex and making love to the woman who aroused his every longing. Ally belonged to the category of women one would have to call unforgettable. He was mad to touch her. But he didn't move, instead saying quietly, "Your hand isn't shaking any more."

"You're here," she said, her eyes alive with emerald light. "Stay for a while." Rafe always had been an intensely strong and reassuring presence.

"You feel the need to be protected?"

"Believe it." She gave a brittle laugh.

Rafe took a quick gulp of the fragrant black coffee, hot and strong the way he liked it, then set the cup down. "I'm picking up a lot of bad vibes here, Ally. You're not going to tell me you're being harassed by some crank? I know it happens to people in the public eye."

She was struck by his perception. She knew she flushed.

"You mean that sort of thing is happening?" he asked, almost incredulously.

"On and off." She tried to appear unfazed.

"Keep talking," he ordered, his strong handsome face turning grim.

She sank back into the sofa opposite him, the light glancing off her beautiful satin dress, making all the little crystals on the strapless bodice twinkle like stars. "I've had letters, phone calls. The calls must be made from public phones. The police can't get a trace on them."

"Someone speaks? A man?" He gave a dark, forbidding frown.

"I'm afraid so, though he seems to use a device to disguise his voice. It's really rather scary."

He stared at her, decidedly the object of any man's desire. "Scary? I'd like to get my hands on him." His voice rasped. "Does Brod know?"

Vigorously she shook her sable head. "You think I'd spoil his wedding? His honeymoon? No way! It's not like this creep is actually doing anything. I've never been stalked. At least I don't think I have." She realised her characteristic blithe self-confidence was breaking down.

For a split second Rafe felt even he couldn't cope with it. "When did it start?" he asked very quietly, his eyes pinned to her expressive face.

Of course she knew exactly. "Four months ago. The channel is very good to me. They've arranged security for me. I have someone to see me to my car."

He let out a hard, tight breath. "No wonder you nearly jump out of your skin when you imagine you see a man's reflection."

"Maybe I'm not quite sober." She tried to make light of it. "I had rather a lot of champagne at the reception. I'm not afraid."

"I think you've proved you are. And why not? This modern world is turning into a jungle. Have you told Fee?"

She rubbed her arms. "I've told no one in the family. Only you. It's an occupational hazard, Rafe. I have to live with it."

His expression was formidable. "This is really bad, Ally. I don't like it at all."

Her mouth trembled. So he still cared something for her. "I have hundreds, maybe thousands of fans who only wish me well, but this guy is something else."

A gust of wind came up and moved the plants on the terrace, causing Ally to lift her hands to her temples. "I thought I'd prefer to stay here rather than a hotel where

I'd be recognised." She leapt to her feet. "Now I'm not so sure. I expect I'm feeling a bit more vulnerable after such an emotional day."

"Sit down again," Rafe said. "Let's face it, Ally, there's a decision to be made. You don't have to spend a single night feeling threatened. Not while I'm around. You mightn't be my Ally anymore but the Kinrosses and the Camerons go back a whole lot of years." Brod looked to him to oversee the running of Kimbara in his absence, the idea that his only sister was in any danger would upset him greatly.

"What I'm offering, Ally, is friendship allied to the age-old tradition of man as a protector. It's the way of the Outback." He tossed off the rest of his coffee, watching her slide back on the couch. "I think what I should do, what Brod would want me to do, is stay overnight. I can sleep on this sofa. Maybe shove the two of them together."

She didn't know what to say, a thousand sensations crystallising into a feeling of great warmth. She also remembered Rafe's tenderness. "Rafe, I don't want you to do that."

"The lady protesteth," he raised an eyebrow, "but I can see relief in those beautiful almond eyes. I don't want to hear any more about it. I'm staying. I won't tell anyone if you don't."

"I imagine it would upset Lainie for days on end." Her gaze flickered to his. Found it sardonic.

"I'm not sure what you're on about as regards Lainie, and I don't actually care. You're nervous about staying here and I don't blame you. I'd just like to run into this guy who's been giving you such a bad time. Are you sure it's not someone you know?"

The police had said the same thing. "You mean,

someone I work with? One of the actors, one of the crew?''

"Take it easy," he soothed, watching her reaction. "Tell me the sort of things he writes. What he says on the phone.''

"Rafe, you wouldn't want to hear it." She slid her heavy hair back from her face.

"So it's a sexual thing?''

"Of course." She glanced away, her high cheekbones stained with colour. "He claims he's in love with me. He can give me everything I need. He likes to say how he's going to do it. I crash the phone down. I've had three different ex-directory numbers but he always finds out. That's not easy to do.''

"And the letters? There aren't any fingerprints?''

She shook her head. "The police have checked all that out.''

"They're taking it seriously?''

"Yes, they are. One of the anchor women from another channel resigned because she was being harassed. I don't like the idea of some nut dictating my life.''

"That figures. You've still got the letters?''

"The police have. They think it's someone who knows me, as well. He certainly knows what I'm wearing on any given day.''

"And you've kept all this to yourself." He had a tight control over his voice.

"I'm trying to be brave, Rafe.''

"Sounds more like you're being foolish. Brod and I could have solved this. You should have told him. You should have told at least one of us.''

"I have," she reminded him. "With Brod there never seemed to be time. I didn't want to spoil anything for him or Rebecca. God knows Rebecca had her bad times with that first husband of hers. I didn't want to stir up any bad memories. I'm glad you're here,'' she finished on a gentle sigh.

"So am I,'' he answered, but his expression was grim. "But I have to tell you in Brod's absence I intend to take over his role. I think we should get some competent woman to come and stay with you until this thing is straightened out. I'm thinking of Janet Massie here.'' He referred to a long-time friend. "You've always liked her and Janet knows how to handle herself. She's been a lost soul since Mick died. Looking out for you will give her something positive to do. And the money would come in handy.''

She kept her eyes down. "Rafe, Janet wouldn't want to come to Sydney. She's never left the bush.''

"Try her. If you want her, Janet will come. Better yet, I'd like to see the guy to confront her. Janet has developed as much muscle as I have.''

"I don't know.'' Yet she felt like going with his instincts. "My apartment isn't much bigger than this one. I'm used to living alone. So is Janet since she lost her husband.''

"Let's talk this through,'' Rafe suggested. "Janet is a good bloke. She's got a great sense of humour. She won't get in your way. It's not forever. As soon as I can settle a few of my own affairs I'd like to conduct a little investigation of my own. The police have enough on their hands. They don't have the manpower.''

"Let me think about it, Rafe,'' Ally pleaded, though she honestly couldn't think of anyone better than Janet to man the fort. Janet was a real character with the proverbial heart of gold. The sort of woman you could pour out your heart to. It would be comforting, too, not to have to come home to a dark empty apartment. At least while this was going on.

She had thought of confiding in Fee but decided against it. Fee being Fee couldn't help turning everything into a great drama. Fee would have told Brod. Francesca. Anyone who had ears. Fee sometimes could be positively unnerving. Francesca, on the other hand, who could always be relied upon to keep her head, lived on the other side of the world. She was just going to have to go along with Rafe's plan.

CHAPTER FOUR

IT WAS ludicrous to think Rafe at six foot three could pass a comfortable night on the couch.

"Why don't you take the bed?" Ally implored. "I don't mind in the least where I sleep."

"Why don't I simply move in with you," he said, his voice laced with heavy sarcasm. "Then you wouldn't be on your own in the dark."

"I don't think you're serious." Her heart rocked at the very thought. She couldn't suppress flashes of how it had been between the two of them. Turbulent bliss. Surely feeling like that could never be lost?

"No, I'm not," he told her bluntly, brushing her with his iridescent gaze. "You're not the woman in my life any more, Alison, my darling." Yet what woman could fascinate him so.

"So, then, who is?" Ally began to shake out the boronia-scented sheets with unnecessary vigour.

"Hey, lady, that's private." Masterfully he took the sheets off her, draping one over the sofa and leaving the other on a chair close by. "What I really ought to do is roll up like a hedgehog."

"I know." She stood there worrying. "You're much too big."

"I've slept in a whole lot worse places. I've actually perfected the art of falling asleep in the saddle. Now, push off," he said, his tone remarkably casual, considering her proximity was like some kind of purgatory to him. Ally was so good at this.

49

She had already taken off her beautiful rose pink bridesmaid gown, replacing it with a tightly sashed brocade robe with satin lapels that matched her eyes. Her polished olive skin glowed in the light. Her curly mane rained down her back and shoulders. Her beauty stunned him. No matter what she had done to him he would never tire of looking at her. He'd created this situation, now he was stuck with it.

"You have to fly home tomorrow," she added, as though it were an outrage to ask him to sleep on the couch.

"Ally, darling, be a good girl and go to bed," he told her, praying for patience. "You can leave the blanket."

"But what about pyjamas?" She continued to hover, wishing she could come up with something that might serve. But there was nothing in this feminine abode.

"Hell, girl, I don't sleep in pyjamas," he drawled. "If it's really cold I might get into a tracksuit. But it's not cold. It's balmy."

"So, what then?" she persisted, radiating concern. "It isn't all that warm at night. This is June. Officially Winter." He had taken off his slate blue jacket, the silver cravat, and unbuttoned a few buttons of his finely pleated white shirt. He looked so wonderful, so vigorous and full of life she was terrified she was going to make a fool of herself.

"Go, Ally." He pointed firmly to her bedroom door. "You've seen me naked. I've seen you naked. There's nowhere else for us to go. Anyway that was a long time ago. But don't panic. I intend to stick to my briefs."

"Right." She drew her robe closer around her, knowing she was outstaying her welcome, but longing for closer contact, the touch of his hands, his mouth, his skin. "Good night, Rafe, dear." She thought she might try to kiss him like a sister but she realised that would be impossible.

"Damn it, Ally, stop it!" he exploded. "And you can forget the dear. I don't think I can cope with it."

"So I've used up all my credit?" She looked at him with sadness in her gaze.

He straightened, staring across the small distance that separated them. The overhead light glanced off his taut, arresting face, accented his strong cheekbones, put a deeper groove in the cleft in his chin. "Can I be honest with you, Ally?"

"Of course." She held the satin lapels of her robe to her throat, starting to look apprehensive.

"You'll always be part of me. Part of my heart. But what I feel for you, what I felt for you, is like a great weight that's dragging me down. I have to get on with my life. I've virtually had no life since you took off and left me. A few affairs that never came off. I know sweet little Lainie imagines herself in love with me but I don't intend to break her girlish heart. I don't like hurting people."

She winced as though he'd hit the rawest nerve. "Are you saying *I* do?"

He looked as her with cool condemnation in his glittering eyes. "Yes, Ally, I am, but I forgive you. Forgive but not forget is my motto. I'm well on the way to being healed so don't just stand there flaunting your warm, sweet body in that gorgeous robe. Go to bed and sleep well. I'll be right outside your door like ghillie Brown with Queen Victoria."

She took a deep breath, trying not to feel deeply wounded. "All right, Rafe." She had some pride, after all. "I do appreciate your staying. I'll be up early in the morning. I'll make breakfast."

He shook his head. "Don't worry about me. Cup of tea and a bit of toast."

"Good night, then," she bid him quietly, turning to walk away.

Good night, Raphael. My golden angel.

Good night, Ally, my torment.

Hours passed. Hours Rafe dozed fitfully, unable to find a comfortable position, unable to fall off to sleep however much he willed it, unable to quiet the tumult in his body, the images of Ally that bloomed in his brain. Finally he pulled the blanket around him and sat in the armchair propping his feet on the footstool Ally had found in the study. God! he thought desperately, wishing his blood was as cool as the breeze that was coming in from the half open sliding-glass doors.

He never could sleep without lots of fresh air. He hated the times he had to stay in hotels. The confinement and that damned air-conditioning. Down the hallway Ally was sleeping the sleep of the innocent, he thought ironically. He could actually hear the quiet rhythm of her breathing. So she hadn't shut the bedroom door. An invitation? He wouldn't put it past her. He fancied he could hear her very heartbeat, causing him to jam his head between his hands to block it out.

Face the horrifying truth, mate. You're still in love with her and there's nothing you're going to be able to do about it. Except not show it. He hadn't survived all the pain to lay his heart wide open again. He would suffer a lifetime denial rather than let Ally treat him like a fool again. Not that she wouldn't like to try it. Tugging on his heartstrings was a part of her. Probably she'd never been totally happy unless she knew what they had would never be over. She had been truly glorious to make love to. His perfect woman. The goddess with feet of clay.

Lainie had given him the news Ally was considering a movie offer. Why not? She was a born actress. A natural. She'd look brilliant on the big screen. She had such a luminescent quality. What was to stop Ally if Hollywood beckoned? He knew she could slip into an authentic American accent. Sound as English as Francesca. Another part of her training. Accents.

He only wished to God this guy who was harassing her would appear on the terrace right now. After he finished with him it was unlikely he'd ever harass Ally again. From down the hallway came a little catch of a moan. She was having a bad dream. He wondered if he should check. Decided not to as her breathing became quiet again. You have to overcome this, sport, he thought wryly, bring your mind to bear on getting to sleep. Mind control is what it's all about. But desire for Ally continued to saturate his blood.

It was late at night. She was in the underground car park, moving urgently towards her car. Arnold the security guard wasn't with her. The lights were too dim. She always thought that. There seemed to be a haze, as well. She thought she smelt cigarette smoke. Cigarette smoke made her ill. She turned her head, casting her eyes around swiftly with false bravado. She was nervous. As nervous as a cat with a Rottweiler in sight. One of the cast, an older woman, told her to always carry a small can of hair spray in her bag. If you couldn't get hold of the illegal mace, hair spray would have to do. Anything to give you a minute to get away.

She was conscious she hated all this. The fear. Why should women walk in fear? It wasn't fair. She could hear her breath whirring in her chest. Her car wasn't far away but she couldn't seem to close the distance. It was almost as though she was walking through water. She tried to increase her pace, approaching a pillar with a big black H on it. She almost passed it only to be confronted by a figure. A nightmare figure. It was wearing a balaclava, a black mask like a storm trooper. She could clearly see the eyes.

She tried to cry out but nothing passed her throat. She was struck dumb by fear. The man in the mask spoke. The voice was muffled by the balaclava over his head. Yet she knew it. It was the same voice that whispered obscenities to her on the phone. She made a move towards him. Hit out. A reflex action that turned into a furious swipe. If only she could claw the mask from his face. So near to him she thought she knew the odour of his sweat. She wasn't going down without a fight. He tried to backhand her but he couldn't seem to connect. She found her voice screaming for help. If she could only hold on someone would come to rescue her.

"You miserable swine! You bully! You coward!"

Now he held his hand over her mouth and she tried to bite it hard. Something was holding her like a winding rope. She kicked and fought, blind with fear and frustration. I have to live through this, she thought. I'm young. I have to find a way to make Rafe love me again. I have so much to live for. She could use her nails. They were long and sharp. Only the hands that were holding her were strong. Too strong for her. She could feel her wild thrashing slowing, slowing, like a woman undergoing sedation.

The nightmare face above her seemed to have disappeared....

She stopped fighting altogether. Sagged.

"Ally, Ally."

The terrible muffled whisper was gone, as well. The voice was deep, bracing, full of command. And, so blessedly familiar.

Rafe.

The certain knowledge jolted her right out of it. She snapped open her eyes.

She was lying in a bed, trussed up like a mummy. Bedclothes. Rafe was staring down at her, his gold hair tousled, holding her firmly by the arms.

"For God's sake, Ally, snap out of it!" he urged. "You're making my blood run cold."

Full consciousness took hold of her clouded brain. She sat up, groaning. "I'm sorry. I'm sorry." She tried to push her own wild mop of hair away from her face. "I was having a nightmare."

"You can say that again!" His voice cracked with irony. "Hell, you were trying to bite me. I had to stop that screaming before the whole building cried rape."

"I'm sorry," she moaned again, kicking out in frustration at the bedclothes that had somehow tied her in a knot.

"Here, let me do that." Roughly he freed her, letting her tumble on her side. The room was white with moonlight. He could see her clearly. She was wearing a nightgown that had long clingy sleeves but the low oval neckline revealed the exquisite slopes of her breasts.

"Do you suppose someone is going to knock at the door?" She wasn't fooling, either.

"Hell, I'm surprised someone hasn't called for the police."

"As bad as that?" She made a supreme effort to pull herself together.

"It would have been if I hadn't muffled most of it. My God, Ally, what were you dreaming about?"

"My phantom stalker," she said bleakly, suddenly punching the pillow. "I was putting up a fight."

"Your bites are specially good. It's a wonder you didn't try to scratch my eyes out."

"I didn't hurt you, did I?" She rolled towards him, tried to grasp his hand. "Heck, you're cold."

Abruptly he withdrew his hand from her warm clasp. "I didn't have time to put on my nightie," he said with heavy sarcasm, his brain telling him to get out of here as quick as he could.

"You don't need to," she said huskily. There was something about a man's bare torso she thought, staring up at him. Broad in the shoulders, tapering to a narrow waist, his chest hazed with golden brown hair that ran in an arrow and disappeared into his dark briefs. Not an ounce of superfluous flesh on him. She was about to reach out and stroke him, but caught herself in the nick of time. "I suppose it was triggered by talking about him, the stalker," she explained.

"I guess so." Why the hell did she have to turn into the beam of moonlight, her body curved invitingly. An erotic vision.

"There was something about the figure in the dream," she confided with a tiny edge of hysteria, "but I've lost it." Her breath fluttered and the neckline of her night-gown moved down further, exposing her breasts as creamy as roses.

"Don't you dare try anything on," he warned her, a dark frown drawing his brows together.

She swung up in mock outrage. She wanted him so badly she was prepared to try anything. "I have no idea what you're talking about," she lied. "You know perfectly well…"

"What? What is it I know perfectly well?" he challenged her.

She surrendered all of a sudden, propelled by her mounting urgency. "I want you, Rafe," she said, her whole body quivering with nerves and desire. "Sometimes I wish I didn't, but I do. I want you to hold me close. I want you to come in beside me."

This nightmare of hers could be no more than trickery, he thought with sudden anger. She was a marvellous actress. "I see." His voice was harsh. "We make love until dawn, then you fly off to Sydney and your brilliant career. Lainie only told me tonight you've been offered some big part in a movie. You didn't tell me."

"I don't know how much I want it." She caught at his hand, held it, despite the fact his fingers had gone rigid as he steeled himself against her touch. "How can you be so cold to me," she implored, carrying his hand to her breast, holding it there so he could feel the chaos inside her. "I know I did something dreadful but can't you try to understand?"

He took his hand back deliberately, his voice heavy with scorn. "Ally, please, no more. I've spent years killing off my feeling for you. Roll over and go back to sleep, I'm not even tempted."

That, when desire was shafting through his body, so hot, so powerful it was agony. In truth he felt electric, out of control.

"I'd say you are a dreadful liar." She confounded him, shaking her head. "You're in as much pain as I am." Again she grasped his arm, arresting him.

She had beautiful hands. How he remembered the way she used them. Delicate long fingers, tantalising nails, hands that could stroke a man's body so sensuously, the yearning became unbearable.

Her magnificent mane of hair burst around her face, her emerald eyes glittered. Her silken rose-tipped breasts were revealed as she leaned towards him. There was even a teardrop shaped like a pearl clinging to her lashes.

So it remained. The wild love of their youth. How could he not be aware of the passion that had always been between them.

"I want you, Rafe." Her lips parted on a shaky breath.

"So what?" he asked with deep cynicism. "The pleasures of the flesh aren't lasting, Ally. You've always done what you want. Now you offer yourself to me because it just happens to suit."

She was beyond pride. The room was filled with his aura, his energy, his scent. "Rafe, stay with me."

"You're mad!" he said bitterly, while his heartbeat hammered right up to his throat. "Mad to ask this of me."

"I need you." It came out as a quick sob. She needed to tell him how much she loved him. How she had always loved him. Always would. She needed...

He was desperate to stop her entreaties. A grown man filled with furious frustrated desire for a woman. He pushed her almost roughly back onto the bed, for the moment forgetting his own strength so her head came into sharp contact with the mahogany bedhead.

"God, what am I doing?" He groaned, his voice full of self-disgust.

Ally, too, was a little shocked, but full of a jagged excitement. She started to rub the back of her head, though in truth the crack had been cushioned by her abundant hair.

"I never knew you were violent." She forced herself to breathe deeply, trying to quiet the flames that were leaping between them like a bonfire about to go out of control. "Rafe?" she whispered as he shoved the bedclothes aside.

"What part are you playing now?" he taunted her. "The innocent virgin? It doesn't suit you. I think you'd better stick with seductress. You know all about that."

She couldn't bear his contempt. "Listen to my heart," she begged him. "It beats for you."

"Ally, you're a bitch. You really are!" he breathed, his mind carried back to the number of times she had whispered those very same words to him…listen to my heart. It beats for you….

He moved then with breathtaking speed, going down on the bed, all six feet plus of him, radiating male energy and power and a dangerous frustration. While her heart did a crazy cartwheel he took possession of her, pulling her into his arms, shaping her body so masterfully he had it perfectly moulded to his.

"Rafe!" Her face flushed as if from a raging fever even as she had an overwhelming sense of coming home.

"Ally. Damn you."

His mouth came down on hers with bruising strength. A punishment. Only to find her lips open and waiting as though she intended to steal the very soul out of him.

Ally. Unchanged. Ally, his obsession.

He flung his arm over her, imprisoning her as he lowered her back against the bed, realising as he was losing himself neither of them were breaking the long feverish kiss. It went on and on. Ally writhing beneath him, while his free hand, the hand that wasn't clutching her riotous hair, moving with power and urgency over her body.

I've thought about this one million times. Thought about it. Fought it.

Rafe moved his mouth blindly across her eyes, her nose, her cheeks. Her skin had the texture of satin. Now his hand closed over her delicate breast inciting the nipple. She moaned, the same little mewing sounds he remembered from before.

He had tried to despise her. A futile exercise.

"Don't hate me, don't hate me," she implored, still effortlessly reading his mind. Still making it so easy for him to caress her beautiful body. Women like her knew how to turn the tables. She was the victim now. He was the man with a heart of stone.

His body tensed, bringing hard muscles into play. Immediately she locked him with her long slender legs. Threw her arms around his neck. "Don't leave me, Rafe."

His heart thudding so loudly it might have been trying to break out from behind his ribs. "You're a witch," he accused her harshly. "A witch and worse."

"But you can't do without me." She stared into his eyes.

He wanted to hurt her as much as she had hurt him. "When it comes to sex, I guess we're perfectly matched." He bent his golden head, burying his face in the curve of her neck while she began to whisper strangely. Little incantations she once told him, Lala Guli, a powerful old aboriginal woman on Kimbara had taught her. The same incantations she had used years ago. Magic. Woman magic. In reality, potent.

The blood roared in his veins like a great tumult of water over a canyon. He lifted her in his strong arms. Hoisted her over him, held her while her hair, that incredible hair, fell, covering them both like a curtain.

Then slowly, tortuously he lowered her against his intemperate body.

He was mad for her. Quite simply mad. One word said it.

Now, witch that she was, was kissing him all over his face. Little fluttery kisses like a butterfly dancing. Kisses that got right under his skin. Tiny traitorous kisses that he had to put a stop to.

He took hold of her head between his two hands, holding her, kissing her until he almost put a stop to her breath. In defiance of everything, his will and his pride. She was Ally. His one and only woman. His desire for her had grown ever more insatiable over time.

So long. So long.

The heat between them was sparking, running like a flame towards dynamite. Rafe drew a deep shuddering breath pushing her nightgown to her waist, lowering his head so he could kiss her swelling breasts, take the fragrant, tightly bunched berries right into his mouth. Too late now to curse himself for his human frailty. Yet he had never felt more powerful, more virile.

"My love, my love!"

Her frenzied little cry sent him totally off balance. She *knew* this had been inevitable. A kind of angry laugh broke from him even as he readied her body to receive him, realising as he entered her, her beautiful face was wet with tears.

Ally woke with a start and leapt to her feet, reaching for her discarded nightgown to cover her nakedness. Her body still bore the imprint of Rafe's, the male scent of him clung to her skin. She thought she remembered exactly how it was, the feeling that poured over them like a king tide, but nothing could match what happened between them last night. Her skin drenched with colour and her eyes blazed in her face. She would remember it all her life.

Afterwards she thought she could never sleep, her body still throbbed and pulsed, but Rafe had lain beside her so quiet, so profoundly thoughtful, she had turned her head into the pillow and, exhausted, had fallen into a deep dreamless sleep. Now she tied her mass of hair into a rough ponytail and hurried down the hallway. The apartment was very still, like there was no one there.

"Rafe?" she cried in earnest. Her normally melodious voice high-pitched with a residue of powerful emotion.

"I hear you."

He was out on the balcony, looking at the streams of traffic that moved over the Expressway spanning the river. Now as he walked back into the apartment looking not the least bit dishevelled but terribly dashing, his eyes moved over her, taking in the stained cheekbones, the brilliant eyes, the way the sunlight rayed through her nightgown, outlining her figure.

"Good morning, darling," he drawled, mockery in his eyes, his attitude, in the very twist of his mouth.

"You shouldn't have let me sleep in." All of a sudden she felt profoundly unbalanced.

"I was about to call you." He glanced casually at his watch. "You have plenty of time."

"I wanted to make your breakfast." Uncertainly she turned towards the galley.

"How charming!" His iridescent eyes glinted. "Actually I attended to myself. A quick shower. Tea and toast."

She'd heard nothing so deeply had she slept. "About last night..." she said in a faraway voice.

"Should be the title of a book, don't you think? A

screenplay. A film starring the glorious, sexy, Ally Kinross. No wonder men worship you.''

By this point she knew exactly where she stood. ''Can't we talk about this, Rafe?'' she begged.

''Darling, no. I must dash off. But I had fun.''

''Fun? Is that what we had?'' She looked at him questioningly, pain in her eyes.

''What do you want me to say, Ally? I'm about to shoot myself. Unrequited love?''

''I meant everything I said.''

''How astonishing!'' He lifted one golden brown eyebrow. ''We didn't *talk* at all, though you had a particularly good time with all Lala's jargon.''

''It's not jargon and you know it. It's ritualistic love magic.''

He laughed, a discordant sound, but attractive. ''Whatever the hell it is, it works. For a time.'' He checked his watch again, stretched with a graceful movement that put her in mind of some lithe big cat. ''Ally, I adore you. Thank you for having me over. Now I intend to stay until it's time for you to leave for the airport. I'll ring the cab and put you in it myself. Then I have to beat it back to my own hotel, pick up my things and settle my account. The Piper is at Archerfield. I'll only be a little late for takeoff.''

She turned her head away to hide her distress. ''You don't *have* to wait for me.'' It was almost as though she had dreamed last night or had their lovemaking existed in another dimension?

''But I intend to.'' He had turned up his sleeves in an attempt to appear more casually dressed when he returned to his hotel. The finely pleated white shirt was obviously a dress shirt but open-necked, long sleeves tucked up, with the beautifully cut slate blue trousers, his gold hair perfectly groomed, he looked more like a movie star than a cattle baron. "You see, Ally," he trod softly past her and pinched her cheek, "I briefly considered treachery but discarded it. I'm taking this harassment problem of yours very seriously. I'm going to get on to Janet this very day and ask her to help us out. Something tells me she'll jump at the chance. I'll arrange for her to fly to Sydney, give her your address and ex-directory number. It might be an idea to write it all down and you can take it from there."

"You'll do this for me?" Her voice was grateful.

"I certainly will. I can hardly forget I once loved you dearly. Anyway you're a Kinross. My best friend's sister. Brod and Rebecca would be deeply disturbed if they knew what's been going on."

"You won't tell them?" she pressed him. "You won't let them know. Not while they're on their honeymoon."

He agreed with a faint niggle of worry. "You must let me act in Brod's stead. But I insist you go to Fee while you have the locks to your apartment changed. I think you should tell her. I expect her to be terribly concerned, but please tell her to leave it to me. Make her understand we don't want Brod and Rebecca caught up in it yet."

"I hate all this," she said. "The terrible unease. I can't get accustomed to it at all."

"It will soon be over," he promised, his expression turning grim. "I have some urgent business that will keep me on Opal for the best part of this week but I'd like to come to Sydney after that and look around for myself. Have a chat to the particular police officer in charge of your investigation. Maybe your bosses, your producer. Why don't you go off and have your shower while I make some coffee. I know you don't like tea."

She nodded. "I hate to drag you into this thing, Rafe. I know better than anybody how hard you work. All your responsibilities."

"Don't worry about it, Ally," he said. "I have the will and the energy and I'll feel a lot better when the whole matter is cleared up. In the meantime I want you to be very, very careful."

"Tell me about it!" A shadow of her luminous smile. "Did you know Fee will have Francesca and David staying with her?"

"Fee told me. So what? I haven't seen it but Brod said your aunt bought herself a great house right on the harbour."

This time Ally gave a genuine laugh. "It's really something. Much too big for one person but you know what Fee's like. She's used to splendour. The ex-countess and all. She has live-in help, a husband and wife, and she intends to entertain a lot. She's been approached by important people in the Arts to give of her enormous experience."

Rafe nodded. "I'm sure she'll enjoy it. A woman like Fee should never retire. I happen to know she adores you and she worships Brod, so take advantage of the situation. Your aunt will always be there for you. She's returning home today, isn't she?" he questioned with a slight frown. Maybe she wasn't.

"Afternoon flight," Ally confirmed. "Fee never can get up in the morning. I expect Fran will want to spend every moment with Grant."

His shapely mouth tightened. "Fran is a beautiful girl and she has all the charm in the world but I hope you're not promoting any romance. I know Fran's your cousin and you're very fond of one another, but an English rose won't transplant easily to the desert. Francesca is a titled young woman. An aristocrat from the other side of the world. Lady Francesca de Lyle. It suits her beautifully.''

''Of course it does,'' Ally said with a return to her usual spirit, ''but she has a Kinross for a mother. Her father doesn't have as much money as you might think. It's been Kinross money that's been allowing Fran to move easily through her privileged world and incidentally helping out the earl.''

Rafe's brows shot up. ''Well then, that's a surprise.''

''It would be a surprise to a lot of people, I guess,'' Ally said simply, ''including Fran.''

''You mean, she doesn't know?'' Rafe gave an incredulous laugh.

''I'm certain she doesn't,'' Ally said. ''Fee didn't intend her to know. Perhaps Fee felt guilty about all the lost years and thought money wouldn't serve. Who knows. All I'm saying is, it's my family who have the money, Rafe. Not the earl. He has the stately pile but it has nearly sent him broke.''

Rafe drew a whistling breath. ''That's a pretty big secret. You think you can trust me with it?'' He challenged her with his iridescent eyes.

''I'd trust you with my life,'' she said. It had the ring of perfect truth.

CHAPTER FIVE

FEE was in wonderful form, enjoying herself enormously. Her mother was one of those women who could go on for hours and hours without ever losing her audience, Francesca thought, torn between love and a lifetime of regrets.

Lady Francesca de Lyle, the poor little rich girl, sent to live with her father after her parents divorced. "A marriage that had started to disintegrate from day one," her father always said. She had suffered and her father had suffered. Victims of Fee's relentless pursuit towards fame. With her many long years in the public eye, the luxurious lifestyle she had led, her fame as an actress, her two prominent marriages, one to a reserved English aristocrat, her father, the other to a handsome, flamboyant vagabond of an American film star who had cast his spell over millions of women around the world, it was only to be expected Fee had many a riveting story to tell. Not only that, she kept changing voices for all the various people she portrayed.

"Such a marvellous raconteur," David murmured, his elegant face full of admiration. "The most beguiling woman I've ever met."

Francesca gave a little wry smile. "Some piece of work," was the way her father phrased it. She tried to push to the back of her mind the sad lonely years when there had been far too many things going on in her mother's brilliant career for her to pay attention to a small daughter. Still I love her dearly, Francesca thought, seeing, as a woman, how her mother and father had been almost totally incompatible.

"Living with your father was like living without conversation," Fee once told her. "The most exciting communication was how the home farms were doing, or how much it was going to cost to fix a section of the blessed roof. Some part of it was always caving in. Decent man that he is, one could scarcely call your father profound." But for a long while he had been kept captive.

Dinner over, Fee got them all moving to the living room for coffee and liqueurs. Fee loved people. Obviously what she couldn't suffer was silence. How very different we are! Francesca realised it more and more with every day. An only child, she had been thrown back on herself for entertainment, relying heavily on her love of reading and roaming her father's beautiful estate.

Like all the de Lyles she was a born country woman. And her love for the land didn't stop at England's green fields. She found her mother's ancestral home, Kimbara, the most thrilling place on earth. The sheer immensity of it, the frightening isolation, the savage beauty and most of all the colourations of the extraordinary landscape, the hot pinks and yellows, the fiery brick reds and the white and black ochres that contrasted sharply with the blazing blue sky. She loved the burnt umber of the great plains, the mile after mile of parallel sand hills breaking to the horizon in a blue sea of mirage.

She'd been ten years old when her mother had first brought her to Australia. "Home" to the great homestead where Fee had been born. A homestead which, far from appearing insignificant in comparison with her father's magnificent Ormond Hall, had a quite extraordinary impact of its own. When she really thought about it, Kimbara stood alone as another fascinating planet might stand alone. All she knew was she loved it. She could even settle there.

An English rose in the desert? She heard Grant Cameron's deep drawling tones.

Hadn't he forgotten this great country of theirs was opened up by settlers from the British Isles? There had been plenty of English roses, Scottish roses, Irish roses, you name them, all mentioned in their history books. Strong, fearless women who had imposed their own kind of civilisation on the Timeless Land. The Kinrosses and the Camerons had their origins in Scotland. There had been powerful women figures in the family. She must remind Grant of that, whenever she saw him again. God, she had really complicated her life allowing herself to fall in love with a man from the Outback.

"Come on, my darlings!" Fee came up, arms outflung. She swept them from the entrance hall into the luxuriously appointed living room, dominated by a wonderful portrait of her at the height of her beauty and fame. It hung in splendour above the Italianate fireplace, a focus for all eyes.

"*Absolutely dazzling,* David thought. The artist had caught her very essence. Passionate, histrionic, wilful, possessed of a boundless inner energy that had driven her brilliant acting career. She was dressed in an exquisite haute couture ball gown of emerald silk, posing on a small gilt and embroidered silk settee that was part of a suite in his brother's Gold Drawing Room. The pose was pure Singer Sargent, Fee leaning forward slightly to display the beautiful curves of her shoulders and bosom. Not a man to take a great deal of notice of women's fashions, David remembered that gown well.

Francesca had not inherited her features or Fee's flamboyant nature. She was a de Lyle. The one who most resembled Fiona Kinross, the star, was her niece, Alison. Both of them had that flamelike quality, a combination of strength and a strange, touching, vulnerability. Alison, too, was making her mark, Fee had told them at dinner, while her niece tried to stop her. Alison had been offered the female lead in an exciting new film. A thriller. David supposed if the film took off Alison would go to America and perhaps never come back. The Kinross women seemed to choose a career before marriage.

Suddenly he felt enormously grateful Fee had retired, although people were always offering her jobs. At the end of the year her biography written by Brod's clever wife, Rebecca, would come out. How far would it go? Whatever her faults Fee wasn't the woman to want to deliberately hurt anyone. He thought of de Lyle, now quietly but contentedly married. How had Fee and his cousin ever got together? They couldn't have been more different. It wasn't as though Fee had been looking for a step up the social ladder. She was a princess in her own country and, let's face it, Fee had brought to her marriage a magnificent dowry. Fee the golden girl with the Midas touch. David suddenly realised he couldn't bear to let her go out of his life. In his mind she was like a ray of glorious sunshine and he so loved the Australian sun.

Ally waited until long after their guests had departed and Francesca and David had said their good-nights. Fee, the habitual night owl, was still as bright as a button, sitting on a sofa, talking over the events of the evening.

"I had mixed feelings about asking Miles and Sophie but it turned out rather well, don't you think?" she asked rather slyly.

"Yes," Ally agreed with a degree of amazement. "Not everyone asks along a ménage à trois, present husband, ex-husband."

Fee laughed. "Honestly why Miles and Sophie broke up, I'll never know. They were a team!"

"Fee, I have something to tell you," Ally interrupted before Fee had a chance to summon up an anecdote about her theatrical friends.

"Darling," Fee patted the sofa beside her, "come here. Of course you can tell me anything you like. There's something on your mind. I've been trying to get it out of you since you arrived."

"It's not about Rafe," Ally answered wryly. She sat down beside her aunt, taking Fee's elegant beringed hand with its knockout brilliant cut seven carat solitaire diamond, a love token from her second husband. "Is this darn thing insured?" Ally rearranged the ring a bit.

Fee shook her head. "I can't keep up with the premium."

"Fee, you're a very rich woman." Ally looked her in the eyes.

"That's because I don't give my money away."

"That's news to me." Ally pecked her affectionately on the cheek.

"Darling, I know what you're getting at, but that's a family secret. De Lyle hated taking my money but I insisted. Francesca had to have the best of everything."

"She only wanted her mum."

"I know." Fee nestled closer to her niece for comfort. "Don't remind me of the egocentric woman I was. Tell me your little problem. Not Rafe, of course. He's a big problem."

"I'm being harassed, Fee," Ally said bluntly.

Fee looked around so nervously an armed intruder

might have found their way through the open French door. "My darling girl. This is terrible." Her voice rang with concern. "One can get a maximum of fifteen years for stalking. Have you spoken to the police? You absolutely must."

"If you promise to sit quietly, I'll tell you," Ally said. Fee had a tendency to turn everything into a play starring herself. Ally had seen it before. It didn't take that long to tell her everything with Fee turned to face her full-on, obviously wanting the dialogue to be two-way but holding off valiantly until Ally had finished.

"My darling, don't think I don't know what you're going through!" Fee exclaimed, pushing a silk cushion out of the way. "There was a time, I'd rather not think of it now, it was pretty scary, that wretched person..." Fee broke off, managing to steer herself back on track. "But we can't *not* let Brod know!"

"Hang on, Fee. I have your promise," Ally reminded her.

Fee shuffled her pretty feet in her beautiful Italian evening sandals. "I never realised what you were about to tell me. This is a terrible thing for a young woman to have to endure. Any woman. No wonder you nipped around to my place. You must stay here. Never leave the house. I can arrange everything. Bodyguards, security people."

Ally placed her hand over her aunt's. "Fee, dearest, I'm going back to the apartment after work tomorrow. I know you want to entertain Fran and David. I've heard about all the outings you've lined up. Fran only has a couple more days before she goes home. I don't want you to worry her with this business."

Fee sat back and gave a deep sigh. "Darling, she loves you. She would want to know."

"She can't *do* anything, Fee and I don't want to spoil her stay with anything unpleasant. David, either. He's looking so much better than the last time I saw him."

"I married the wrong cousin." Fee made a wry face.

"That's okay. David was married himself at the time."

Fee thought hard for a moment. "I suppose he was. He's so fond of me. That's the final irony. His mother, God rest her soul, always treated me like a stampeding rhino let loose in the castle. So you're going to leave this all up to Rafe?"

Ally nodded. "Janet Massie will be with me tomorrow night."

"What help would another woman be, darling?" Fee asked doubtfully.

"You haven't seen Janet." Ally smiled. "She's a great character, she's built like a barrel. She ran a cattle station single-handedly after her husband died. You'd have to stomp over Janet to get to me and by then you'd probably be bleeding to death."

Fee was impressed. "So this Janet is going to be your shadow until Rafe arrives?"

"Something like that." Ally nodded.

"If you ask me, the man is still madly in love with you." Fee the expert in such matters sounded utterly convinced.

"Even if that were true, I've convinced him totally I'm not marriage material. He needs someone he's certain is always going to be there."

"Not the little Mary Poppins character, Lainie Rhodes?" Fee gasped. "Why, darling, she fades into insignificance beside you. Though I have to say she's very much more attractive than she used to be but she still puts me in mind of an exctitable…"

"Puppy." Ally uttered a low groan. "Rafe used to say exactly the same thing."

"Darling, I think I need a drink to soothe my nerves." Fee went into a sort of foetal crouch.

"Not if you don't want to wake up with a hangover?" Ally was unmoved. "You know you're off to the Blue Mountains in the morning."

"Forget the Blue Mountains!" Fee swung upright, her rich resonant voice booming with outrage. "I can't possibly go away and leave you."

"Well, good for you," Ally responded, patting her aunt's hand. "But, Fee, it isn't as though this person has ever shown his face. He gets his kicks out of sick letters and obscene phone calls. I'd be really worried if he decided to send around six dozen pizzas. No, you go, Fee. Rafe thought you should know."

"Of course I should know!" Fee flared. "With your father dead, I'm head of the family. Nothing wrong with a bit of tradition."

"Rafe also thought we should keep this strictly between us," Ally added meaningfully.

"All right." Fee gave in with reluctance. "But I'll have Berty," she referred to the husband in her Dynamic Duo team, "drive you right to the door of the studio. I could never ever forgive myself if something happened to you."

It came out with such incredible drama, Ally leaned over to kiss her aunt resoundingly.

"Nothing is going to happen to me, old girl."

Fee laughed. "My darling, you'll be an old girl in time."

"I very much hope so." Ally felt a little prickle of fear run down her spine. "Janet will be there to keep an eye on me and the apartment and Rafe wants to do a little investigation of his own. He'll be here in a few days.''

"Thank God for the Camerons!" Fee breathed. "Crossing either of them would be like crossing Crocodile Dundee. You do know our ancestor, Cecilia Kinross, loved Charlie Cameron not Ewan Kinross the man she married.''

"Perhaps they were all under the weather,'' Ally suggested. "The Scots love a wee drop of Highland malt.''

"That they do,'' Fee agreed fervently. "You're a really good actress, my darling. For what it's worth, fractionally better than I was at your age, but I can't help thinking you missed a glorious opportunity when you let Rafe Cameron slip through your fingers. My best advice to you, based on wide experience, is, go to bed with him. Nothing like bed to cement a relationship. I have my darling daughter to prove it.''

When she slept it was to dream. Fragmentary dreams tumbling one on the other born of the late-night conversation with Fee about the stalker. She was always in some dark place waiting for him to come for her, helpless, at the end of her resources, waking herself up moaning only to fall back into the same dream. She would have emerged wild-eyed, only towards dawn her dream turned to the remembered rapture of earlier years when she and Rafe were inseparable. When Rafe's mother and father had been alive, welcoming her to Opal like her second home. Home really. She had never tasted happiness at Kimbara since her mother had left vowing to gain custody of her and Brod in time but facing an enormous uphill battle against their father's power and influence. They had never seen their mother again, heartbroken children with a father who was a commanding near stranger.

For all of her childhood and adolescence Brod and Rafe had been her heroes. Every time she hugged one, kissed one, she hugged and kissed the other. She adored both of them from infancy. Her brother and her brother's best friend, Rafe Cameron. Five years separated her from her heroes, consequently she had happily taken over the role of little sister. Until, as such things happen, she and Rafe had fallen in love. Then the whole landscape changed and the sweetness of affection, the unshakeable childhood bond became a love so overwhelming it became too much for a young girl's heart to hold. Not that Rafe had ever made her miserable demanding more than she could give him. Even as a boy Rafe could have written the book on self-control. Rafe was very honourable indeed and she had the powerful security of knowing she mattered deeply to him. Rafe, her perfect knight. But they were passionately in love.

Behind her closed lids, half-waking dream sequences stole into her mind...the summerhouse her grandfather had built on the banks of the creek that meandered through Kimbara's home gardens. It was there Rafe had kissed her for the first time as a woman, not a little girl....

There was a party on at the homestead. Past midnight it was in full spate. Her father was entertaining some visiting Asian prince who had taken a fancy to playing polo and bought several of Kimbara's excellent polo ponies. She could see all the lights blazing through the house flowing out onto the gardens. She could hear the music and the laughter, drown in the heady sweetness of jasmine that smothered the white lattice walls of the summerhouse. The night was marvellous with a huge copper moon that spread its radiance all over the desert landscape.

She was sixteen and the tiniest little bit tipsy. Rafe had gone off to get her a cold drink but she had sneaked a glass of fine champagne from one of the waiter's trays, quaffing it quickly, loving the taste and the bubbles, the way they filled her mouth, then the sensation of stars exploding inside her.

"Hey, Ally!" Rafe came back and saw her with the champagne flute, his expression very much big brother.

"Don't be a spoilsport!" she laughed, loving the sparkle that had settled on her. Loving him. She was moving onto the terrace intent on the night, running across the lawn, full of her first intoxication, with responsible Rafe in pursuit. She was breathless by the time she reached the summerhouse, feeling pure joy she had managed to beat him. Him with his long legs and superb male athleticism. Still laughing she held on to a white pillar for support, fragrance in her nose, jasmine flowers catching in the long cloud of her hair. She was wearing a green silk taffeta dress to match her eyes, a new dress, a beautiful grown-up dress, a present from Aunt Fee who lived halfway across the world but never forgot her.

Rafe laughed, too. A lovely indulgent laugh that would be forever in her ears.

"Just look at you," he teased.

"What do you see?" In an instant she was sober, taken over by some unstoppable emotion, an intensity of awareness, suddenly years older. Different.

"I see a sixteen-year-old with the giggles," he said in the same teasing ways but something didn't fit. An edge.

"I only had one glass!" She made an effort to defend herself.

"I know, but you're not having another," he clipped off, already twenty-one and a man. "Time to go back now, Ally. We can't leave the party."

"Why not?" She was full of mischief, a sense of a woman's power. "Who's going to miss us?"

"I'd hate to see you get into trouble," Rafe, long used to Stewart Kinross's severe ways, retorted. "You know what your father is like."

"Perfectly." Suddenly tears pricked behind her eyes. "Loving me and showing me off are two different things. I'm just a possession in my father's world, Rafe. You know that. God help me if I were plain or stupid."

Rafe sighed in tacit agreement, holding out his hand. "Let's go back, Ally." He sounded kind and tender but her blood was fired.

"I absolutely refuse to. And you can't make me." She lifted her face to him with the old childhood dare.

A curl of a smile touched his mouth. "Oh, yes, I can, Ally Kinross. I can pick you up and carry you anywhere. Anytime."

"Dear, darling, Rafe, why don't you do it?" she challenged, seeing the sudden glitter in his eyes, overjoyed he was responding despite himself.

"I'm joking, Ally," he said sternly just to prove it. "Don't make it hard for me."

"Come on Rafe, it's Ally," she said. "Nobody looks after me better than you do." Something sweeter than the jasmine, more powerful than the moonlight surged through her veins. She moved towards him in total silence. Walked right into his arms.

"I love you, Rafe," she said with exquisite pleasure. Words of endearment she had used all her life but never with the unmistakable depths of a woman.

"Ally!" He turned away his splendid head with its

thatch of golden hair, but not before she saw torment hone his features.

"I love you," she repeated, never quite completing the word as he acted like lightning sweeping her into his arms in the most wonderful way imaginable, masterful, romantic, all she had ever dreamed of, his beautiful mouth swooping down to cover hers, warmly, deeply, searchingly, raging with desire. It was simply…a revelation. Heaven.

Afterwards neither of them spoke as though each recognised nothing would be the same between them again. She wasn't his "little chick" any longer. His responsibility. The chick had found wings….

Ally came completely awake, still savouring Rafe's phantom kiss on her mouth. She fancied she even had the scent of him on her skin, the marvellous maleness. She was as needy of him now as she had been then, but in seeking to distance herself from him to gain some perspective on what was happening in their unique relationship she had only succeeded in distancing herself from him completely. If only she'd had a mother to advise her, to sort her out, to help her get a handle on her tumultuous emotions. She realised now Rafe had kept a tight control on his own desire, but then Rafe was five years older, heir to a great historic station and well used to handling responsibility from boyhood. On that score alone they'd been helplessly mismatched.

It was after Rafe's parents had been killed so tragically they had consummated their love. Rafe trying to bury his grief in the rapture her body gave him. She had been awesomely good at offering him forgetfulness, aching for him, aching for lost relationships, the fine man and woman who had fostered her and shown her so much affection. Maybe if Sarah Cameron had lived Ally would have been Rafe's wife today but she'd had no mother figure to call on then and she, too, was missing Rafe's parents terribly.

Is it any wonder she made so many youthful mistakes.

Ally was up early to see the family off. She knew they planned to spend the day in the beautiful Blue Mountains less than an hour's drive from Sydney. The whole area covering some five hundred square miles was famous for its tourist attractions, taking its name from the early settlers because of the marvellous bluish haze that hung over the mountains. Though it looked magical the haze was caused by fine drops of eucalyptus oil in the atmosphere, the heavily wooded slopes being covered with eucalypt trees. Fee had a great friend who lived in the beautiful township of Leura with a very grand garden, so that was an additional attraction.

Ally had just started breakfast prepared by Polly, the female half of the Dynamic Duo—Ally suspected quite correctly Berty and Polly weren't their real names at all, but some invention of Fee's—when Francesca entered the morning room, her lovely serene face lit up with a smile.

"You know Mamma had this room decorated to look almost exactly like our trellised orangerie at Ormond."

"Sweetheart, I know that," Ally said, tipping back her head to look at the fabric-tented ceiling. "What a pity you're not going to inherit the stately pile."

"It's a pile, all right." Francesca bent down to kiss her cousin's cheek, then took a wheelback chair opposite her. "I don't know how it hasn't sent poor Papa broke. It passes to my cousin, Edward, you know, unless I produce a male heir. I don't mind, really. I don't need that kind of inheritance. The upkeep is killing and it's dreadfully cold. I'll settle for Mamma's view of Sydney Harbour." She looked out the open French doors to the balustraded terrace and beyond that the dazzling blue waters of arguably the most beautiful harbour in the world. "Oh, I wish I could stay!"

"So do I!" Ally looked back. "We'd make a wonderful team, we could go everywhere together. It would be such a pleasure to have you."

"I can see it, too, but I have my P.R. job waiting for me back in London."

"Surely you don't have to go back to resign?" Ally poured her cousin a cup of coffee. "You could easily find something here. That patrician face. That patrician voice. Lady Francesca de Lyle ain't bad, either," Ally joked. "Besides, I know you want to stay."

"*That* obvious, is it?"

"It's a woman thing, love. We always know. Actually, I've been working on a plan."

Francesca gave her cousin a speaking glance. "Trouble is, I don't think Grant would ever buy it."

"Why do you say that?" Ally pretended to be shocked. "You don't know the plan yet."

Francesca put out a hand to cover Ally's. "I love it the way you're always thinking of me, but Grant knows how his brother suffered after you left. He's vowed never to make the same mistake."

Ally glanced away, nibbling at her lip. "I was the one who made the mistake, Fran."

"So why don't you tell Rafe that?" Francesca urged.

Ally shook her dark head. "I made a fool of him so he can't and won't forgive me. You don't know those Camerons. They're far too proud."

"Maybe that's just a front?" Francesca asked hopefully. "I know I could get Grant to fall in love with me."

"Sweetheart, as it happens, any man could fall in love with you," Ally said laconically. "I'm certain Grant recognises you for the lovely young woman you are but as a realist he sees you were born into a world infinitely different from an isolated Outback cattle station. Maybe he thinks you couldn't survive in such an environment. Come to think of it, it is a big ask."

"But, Ally, I'm an outdoorsy girl," Francesca said firmly, but not loudly. Polly was due with her breakfast.

Ally rolled her eyes. "Darling, roaming your father's green fields and rolling hills, is a far cry from losing yourself in a killer wilderness. And it is a killer, Fran. Make no mistake. There have been plenty of fatalities to prove it from the early explorers to overseas adventurers who think they can conquer the Wild Heart."

"*You* love it," Francesca maintained. "You grew up on Kimbara. I fell in love with it at age ten. I'm a Kinross, too. On my mother's side."

"Sure you are!" Ally saluted her with her coffee cup. "So what you have to do is change Grant's perception you're not a terribly suitable candidate for Outback wife. It's up to you to make it all happen."

"Ditto!" Francesca smiled.

CHAPTER SIX

JANET MASSIE arrived that same day and immediately slotted in. Though there were thirty years and more between them she and Ally fell into an easy rapport. Both were Outback women, after all.

"You leave it to me, love," Janet told Ally firmly, "no one will go bothering you with me around. What's the world comin' to? It's not manly to harass a young woman. It's a coward's role. Rafe is worried about you. Remember how he solved who was heading up that cattle duffing gang in '96? With a bit o' luck he'll be catching this fella who's been bothering you. Right bastard he is, love, pardon my French. Just let him try and hide from Rafe."

The thing was he'd been doing a very successful job of it, Ally thought.

The next morning when Janet went to collect Ally's mail her attention was directed to a long yellow office-style envelope on which someone had printed Ally's name and address. It wasn't neat. It stuck out jaggedly like a threat. Janet badly wanted to open it and read what it said herself. She couldn't stand the idea of Miss Alison of Kimbara Station, a real lady, being in this kind of trouble. It must be a dreadful strain, but it wasn't her place to rifle through Ally's mail no matter what it was.

Mercifully, Rafe was flying in midafternoon. He would know what to do. Rafe for all his gentlemanly ways was as tough as tempered steel.

*   *   *

"How many more takes before we finish?" Ally asked the show's director, Bart Morcombe, testily and she wasn't testy often. "Why can't Matt ever get his lines off?"

"Because his tiny brain keeps getting in the way?" Zoe Bates who played the affable wife of the local pub owner in the series, suggested.

Morcombe, looking decidedly frazzled around the edges, tried to soothe his star. It was most unusual for Ally to get this uptight, but then she had a lot on her mind lately. They all had with Ally being harassed. It affected every single one of them. Except Matt Harper who had grown up in a very tough neighbourhood and was very nearly punk. "The thing is he's not as professional as you, Ally, and he doesn't have your photographic memory."

"He's an imbecile, that's why," Zoe, who had a pounding headache, cut in. "It's all that coffee."

Morcombe looked at her thoughtfully, scratching his head. "I thought coffee was good for you? Isn't that what they're telling us these days. Anyway it doesn't help much griping, Zoe. We have to keep telling ourselves Matt has gone over big with the viewing public. Our ratings are sky-high. Ally and Matt generate sparks on the small screen."

"'Struth, I thought he was gay!" Zoe snorted beneath her breath, though there was no evidence to support her supposition. Most people in the business tossed the idea around because Matt Harper, an extremely good-looking young man rarely had a girlfriend in tow. His dangerous wrong-side-of-the-tracks looks had won him a lead role in Ally's series. He'd had no training whatsoever, nevertheless he had a definite brooding presence on screen that translated into fireworks.

Without really liking him Ally had tried to help him in all sorts of ways for which he always appeared grateful in his highly defensive fashion, but sometimes, like today, she felt like jamming the script down his throat. Bart was too soft on Matt when he was known to be pretty scathing with lesser lights when it came to getting things right.

It was nearly five o'clock in the afternoon and they'd been hard at it since their 6:00 a.m. call.

Matt eventually sauntered back from his dressing room and gave them all a what-the-hell-are-you-looking-at-me-for look.

"What's taken you so long?" Bart surprised them all by barking.

"I've been teasing my hair." Matt had insolence down to an art form.

Ally exhaled sharply. "Do you think we can wind up this scene, Matt? I'm really tired."

"Sure, princess." He gave her a smile that displayed perfect teeth courtesy of the studio. "Don't have a nervous breakdown. If you all just relax I might be able to remember my lines."

"*Please* do, Matt," Ally pleaded.

He looked down at her, not tall but looking very strong. "I love it when you beg."

The scene called for Matt, the town's angry young man, to come into Ally's surgery, aggressive and slightly drunk.

Matt did it in a single take.

They were just wrapping the episode up when Bart's senior assistant, Sue Rogers, came rushing in like a small tornado. "God, the most exciting man I've ever seen in my life is outside talking to the boss. I tell you he's better than Redford in his prime."

"Oh, I don't think so." Zoe gave a languid wave. "I see you're not wearing your glasses. No one but no one looks like Redford."

"Just see how you react!" Sue sounded faintly hysterical. "He's big and tall and lean and he's got hair a woman would spend a fortune on. I tell ya it's pure gold!"

"Could be a hallucination," Zoe suggested, getting her gear together. "It's been a rough day."

Ally was the only one who knew exactly who it was. It had to be, from that description. Rafe. He'd finally arrived but she never thought he would come to the studio to collect her. Now he was here and her heart rose in her breast like a bird taking flight. She was desperate to see him.

"It'll be a friend of mine," she told them, smiling in Sue's direction. "Rafe Cameron."

"Lordy, lordy, I think I'm going to faint." Sue pretended to stagger. "This is *the* Cameron, the cattle baron?"

"One and the same."

"There!" Sue rounded on Zoe. "What did I tell you? I knew he was someone special. The walk! Boy, oh, boy, stand tall. The scent of the great outdoors! The cattle baron comes over loud and clear."

"I'd like to meet him." Bart sounded fascinated.

"Thank you very much but I'm on my way." Matt spoke rudely, staring hard at Ally. "From the look on your face you really fancy him?"

"Rafe is a sort of a big brother." Ally deftly hid her annoyance. It was none of Matt's business. "With my own brother away on his honeymoon, Rafe wants to look into this harassment business."

"You don't think the cops are doing enough?" Matt

couldn't keep the snarl out of his voice. "They gave me a bad enough time."

"A good thing you can't *write*." Zoe's voice was flat and unkind. Matt Harper brought out the worst in her but even she didn't see Matt as Ally's tormentor.

"What is that supposed to mean?" Matt marched right up to her, his black eyes on fire.

"Nothing, Matt, just a silly comment." Ally checked him by putting her hand on his arm and clutching it hard. "It's OK, OK."

"I take it back," said Zoe with a little shudder.

Matt seemed to quieten, looking down at Ally's elegant, long-fingered hand on his arm. "You're a real lady, Ally, you know that. The *only* one I ever met in my life."

"Didn't you say you were going, Matt?" Bart asked, not wanting any trouble. He tried to take it easy with Matt, damned near raised as a street kid, but he was an arrogant little bastard and he had a mean temper.

That wasn't about to happen. Before Matt could make a move, Rafe walked onto the set accompanied by the boss of the station, Guy Reynolds, a top executive with the national channel.

"Now I know what you mean about the golden boy aura?" Immediately Zoe turned to whisper to Sue. She was highly impressed but Matt's face took on an extra hard edge.

"God, the cattle baron born with a sterling silver spoon in his mouth," he said with amused contempt. "I bet he's got a handshake that could crack coconuts."

Ally shrugged lightly. "Why don't you stick around and find out?"

They all focused on Rafe Cameron as he approached. A full head taller than Reynolds, he was dressed casually in beige trousers, an open-necked shirt and a classic blazer, but his height, his walk, the perfectly coordinated body, the tanned golden skin and the mane of shimmering gold hair, lent him a powerful drawing power. All of a sudden the familiar set seemed to teem with light.

Up close they saw the authority, the *real* authority, the high intelligence in the iridescent eyes, the way little sun crinkles radiated out from their corners, etched in white. A cattle baron if ever there was one.

They could all see how he would look astride a horse, a bandanna around his neck, a rakish akubra pulled down over his eyes. It took all of them a few moments more to realise they were staring. Even Ally who had loved him all her life couldn't take her eyes off him.

Matt didn't get a chance to leave. Introductions were made all round. Rafe was as charming as ever, so charming the cast and crew appeared to be exulting in his presence and his easy, friendly ways. Even Matt smothered his aggressions opening up unexpectedly to the sheer manliness of their visitor, the commanding aura that made for respect.

All frustration with the long day seemed to fall away. Though it was easy to see Rafe Cameron could, if the occasion demanded it, be extremely formidable, a man to be reckoned with, if he liked and approved of you, if you did nothing to harm Alison Kinross, he couldn't be nicer. Even when he put out his hand to shake Matt's, Matt hadn't shied away from it, rather he look flattered.

Twenty minutes later Rafe and Ally were out on the road joining the peak traffic, Ally driving her small BMW.

"So what did you really make of my work mates?" She flashed him a glance, the golden carved profile.

"Pleasant people for the most part," he observed. "But you never can tell."

Ally surrendered to a deep sigh. "The police questioned everyone, as you know. They spent most of their time questioning poor Matt. I believe there's a little file on him downtown. Nothing terribly serious. Years ago when he was a kid, but it all sticks."

"I'd say the guy's had a hard life." Rafe knew all about hardships. "He's like a wound-up coil."

"A terrible life!" Ally confirmed. "In and out of homes. I don't know that I like him. I try, but he makes it difficult for all of us. I have to make allowances."

"What he wants is to start caring about himself before he can start caring about anyone else," Rafe said. "He probably has a poor self-image. I damned near felt like offering him a job. That usually straightens these troubled young guys up. I've seen really bitter kids nobody cared about turn into different individuals when they're given a bit of responsibility."

Ally knew Opal Downs worked in with a welfare program for troubled youth. Rafe had taken it on board after he was approached. Her father had refused point blank.

"The land works its magic," Rafe said. "Being around horses. I don't think Harper's at home with the acting business."

"Just a way to make money," Ally said. Matt had told her that a thousand times. "The strange thing is, he has a decided screen presence. The talk is, believe it or not, people love to talk, Matt's gay."

Rafe gave her a very straight look. "No, he's not, Ally. No matter the rumours, or how they got started. I'm quite sure he fancies himself in love with you."

The traffic was too heavy for Ally to take time off to stare at him. "Wha-a-t?" she cried. "Matt hasn't looked sideways at me, Rafe. Not ever. We play a part. It's called acting.''

"Obviously the camera sees what *you* don't," he said crisply.

"I don't believe this." Ally shook her head. "Matt has no girlfriend…"

"Maybe he's focused on *you*." Rafe, who had gone to the studio deliberately to size up the people Ally worked with, began to speak his thoughts aloud. "Let's think about this. Maybe he's allowing the rumours to circulate. Maybe it suits him. Protective cover. Maybe he doesn't know what to do with his passion. You're Ally Kinross. You have a *name*. A privileged background. You're a heroine to him in a way, but he's afraid of you. And how does he overcome his fear? His shame in his own background? He harasses you."

Ally's hand gripped the wheel in rejection of Rafe's theory. "It's not true, Rafe. We've worked together for quite a while. Heck, he's right under my nose. He had to endure being spoken to by the police for nearly half a day."

"Do you think the police don't know what they're about?" he countered. "The last person you suspect might be all right for the late night movie, but most crimes against women are committed by men close to them. Ex-husbands, ex-lovers, jealous boyfriends, men they come into contact with in the workplace. Men who become obsessed with them. Unfortunately for him Harper does have a police file. We all regret the fact he had to grow up in a violent environment but Harper could have a demon in him and don't you forget it."

He timed his departure, waiting until they pulled out of the car park. The woman was driving. That struck him as funny. The big cattle baron actually allowing a woman to *drive!* Something he never did. Women had no feel for machinery, no road sense. They were rotten drivers. Men were the masters of the world.

Except, for a woman, Ally Kinross was special. Rich, well-born, sexy and very beautiful. He'd give anything if only she would look his way, but that wasn't going to happen. Not with guys like the millionaire boyfriend around. How did these people get to have so much money, anyway? So much power. He had none and his breeding was questionable, as well. Hadn't his slatternly mother taken the trouble to tell him early. "You're not Danny's kid." He hadn't understood then but he did by the time he was seven and already into petty crime. Anyway, Danny's real brood wasn't handsome. Being handsome had earned him good money. Some silly bitch had stopped him in a shopping centre one day and asked him if he'd like to get into modelling, maybe even a TV show. It was unbelievable the way she made it all sound.

"Sign up and leave it to me!"

He had. His looks had even been improved especially since they got his teeth fixed. The perfect white flashing smile. What he hadn't expected was for the silly bitch to fall in love with him. She had to be damned near forty and he hated the colour of her brittle blonde hair. But Ally Kinross! Thunderbolts on sight! Ally the untouchable. That was when he decided to punish her.

Send her letters. Phone calls. It was extraordinary the thrill they gave him. The feeling of power over her. Clever him. He was clean as far as the cops were concerned.

He knew where Ally lived. He had her latest ex-directory number though it wouldn't be so easy to get the next if she changed it. He knew all about the brother's wedding though he hadn't followed her to Brisbane. He knew about the aunt in the great big mansion on the harbour. Now he knew about the boyfriend. The Greek god cum cattle baron.

He had to know what was going on between Ally and her old buddy. Somehow he knew in his bones Cameron was a dangerous new element. But then, all his life he'd enjoyed playing wild games.

When they arrived at Ally's apartment block she ran her car down towards the underground car park, pausing for a moment to activate the huge security door. With Rafe beside her she was spared all sense of nervousness. She knew he was wrong about Matt Harper. It came as a bit of a surprise. Rafe was an excellent judge of men. Obviously he wasn't letting anyone off his list.

On the way home she learned he had already spoken to the detective assigned to her case. The sad fact was the police had no evidence on anyone. They were waiting for whoever was harassing Ally to make a mistake. No one wanted an actual confrontation but the possibility had to be addressed.

Janet was waiting with the yellow envelope. Rafe took it from her, opening it up carefully with the paper knife she passed him.

"Is your name Ally Kinross?" Ally asked him wryly.

"Yes, is it," he replied, his eye glued to a single sheet of ordinary white typing paper, the contents not ordinary at all. Written in misshapen block letters it was ugly, melodramatic, scary.

"What does it say?" Ally sat down hard, her whole body vibrating with upset.

Rafe waited a moment before he answered. "There's something here that might be checked out by an expert."

He ran a finger along his clean-cut jaw line. "An odd kind of speech pattern common to all the communications. It could be feigned, again the obvious misspelling could be, too."

"Matt can spell," Ally said with relief, knowing Rafe's doubts about Matt. "The police checked that out."

"You mean you have someone already. What a blessing!" Janet visibly brightened.

"Rafe suspects everyone," Ally said.

"So would you if you had any sense." His golden brown brows were drawn together in a heavy frown.

"So what does it say?" Ally repeated. "Am I going to get to know?"

He laughed shortly, no amusement in it. "It's not that interesting." Rafe went to refold the letter to put it back in the envelope when he checked abruptly, a decided glint coming into his eyes. "Well, well, well." He focused on the yellow envelope. The back flap had been reinforced with a strip of transparent tape as the glue wasn't all that effective. "Maybe our friend has left a calling card, after all?"

"Tell me, Rafe," she begged. "I feel ill."

He passed her the envelope. "Notice anything under the tape?"

Immediately the sick feeling dropped away. She looked back at him, her whole expression sharpening. "If I'm not mistaken that's a tiny hair. Maybe the sort of hair off a man's wrist."

"Exactly." Rafe took the envelope back from her. "I'll hand this over to the police first thing in the morning. I might even give Detective Mead a ring."

"We're talking DNA?" Ally's expression returned to brooding.

"Hasn't it revolutionised crime fighting?" Rafe nodded. "I'm certain we might get something from this."

"That's wonderful!" Janet beamed. "Now both of you have to eat. Are you staying to dinner, Rafe?"

"As long as you don't try feeding me peanut butter sandwiches." He smiled at her, harking back to a time Janet had done just that. "Unless you'd like to go out?" He glanced across to Ally, seeing her deepening expression. "No one needs to cook."

"You know that's a great idea," Janet said with enthusiasm, "but I won't come along. There's an old movie with Robert Mitchum in it I want to see. Fancy restaurants are for the young and well-dressed."

"Maybe I'd better change." Rafe gave his open-necked shirt an amused glance.

Ally shook her head. "You look fine." He looked wonderful. She would never tire of looking at him.

"Tell you what." Rafe stood up. "I'll go back to my hotel and then I'll pick you up around seven-thirty. It will give you time to relax a bit. Run a bubble bath." As he said it he had an instant vision of her beautiful body barely concealed by glistening foam. "I have one or two calls to make." One to Mead, he thought but didn't say. "Victoria's suit you?" He named a top restaurant.

"You'll be lucky if you get a table," Ally warned. "It's usually booked well ahead."

"I'll get one," he said almost idly.

Janet laughed, her faded blue eyes crinkling with wry amusement. "I bet he will."

With Rafe back in her life, even if he was only looking after her welfare, Ally came alive. She had her scented bubble bath with foam spilling everywhere, relaxing her body in the fragrant, blue-tinged water. Her blood was running like quicksilver as excitement surged through her veins.

The memory of the night they had spent together, that extraordinary night of Brod's and Rebecca's wedding, had stayed with her with absolute clarity. The pounding force of their passion, the desperate hunger that had plagued them both endlessly totally assuaged. Afterwards she had felt peace but Rafe had lain so quietly, arms raised, his hands locked behind his golden head. It couldn't have been plainer. Their passion was mutual. What went on in Rafe's mind kept them apart.

Why, oh, why, had Lainie decided to tell him all about the film role she'd been offered, Ally agonised. It was her own fault mentioning it. Telling Lainie Rhodes anything was like hiring a loudspeaker. She hadn't even read the script yet but Lainie had obviously made it appear she was on the verge of accepting. Fame came before love. Alison Kinross's career was everything. Even Fee was convinced she was going to take the role. Everyone in the business said it was inevitable she would move to the big screen.

"A face made for the movies," Bart always said. What he didn't know was her so-called career had brought her no great joy. The excitement, the satisfaction levels had declined early. The underlying reason was she didn't live for acting. It was Fee who fell in love with her roles. Fee who had found her career on the stage utterly fulfilling. Even to the exclusion of her family. It wasn't Fee who had raised her beautiful little daughter. Fee had been locked into her Art.

Ally had met Francesca's father, Lord de Lyle only twice in her life, found him wholly different from her aunt, even different from his own cousin, David, but no one had disputed he hadn't tried very hard to be a good caring parent.

No one could make up for the absence of a mother. She and Brod had lived with that loss. Fee was born lucky. She's been given the blessed opportunity to get to know her beautiful daughter all over again. It was the strong resemblance between herself and Fee that was always remarked on. Was it any wonder, then, Rafe had come to believe any relationship between them was unworkable. Ally Kinross was set to follow in her famous aunt's footsteps.

When Rafe returned with a box of Belgian chocolates for Janet, Ally met him at the door, the two of them calling a good-night to Janet who had made herself comfortable in an armchair, turned on the television and gleefully opened the delicious assortment. Janet just loved chocolates and these were the very best.

For dinner Rafe had changed into a beautifully cut dark grey suit with a white-collared blue and white striped shirt and a ruby silk tie. For a man who spent most of his life in riding gear he had great taste. Not only that, he had the tall lean body to show clothes off. Ally was pleased now she had worn a new outfit in textured silk. She looked good in black. It was chic, it was elegant, it was sexy. And tonight she was relying heavily on her sex appeal. Sex was a woman's not so secret weapon and she had to come armed if she wanted to convince Rafe she was still necessary in his life.

The maître d' led them to their table, which Ally realised was one of the best in the room. Other diners looked on, absorbing the fact that was Ally Kinross, the TV star, but who was the amazing man beside her? He was clearly someone. He had the looks of a film star but a quite different aura. Absolutely extraordinary. He filled the room like some great beautiful golden thoroughbred.

"Like a martini?" he asked with easy charm.

"I'd enjoy that very much. It's been an awful day, an awful tiring day."

"You don't look the least bit tired," he told her. He could have said you look dazzling, but didn't. Ally made a black dress look the ultimate in sex appeal.

"Aah, that comes with clever make-up," she responded lightly.

"I've seen you without it."

His eyes were so distinctly sensuous, so sexually disturbing, she burst out, "You've seen me..."

"Leave it there, Ally." He seemed to shake himself out of it, picking up the wine list.

"Very well, Rafe," she answered with mock obedience. "But we did have our good times."

"Looking back, yes." His expression unmistakably tightened.

"I seem to do a lot of it these days." She gave a genuine sigh. "Looking back."

He glanced at her over the top of the wine list. "That might get you into trouble, Ally. I'm following the sign post. Straight ahead."

"I just can't see you and Lainie," she offered dryly.

"As it happens, neither can I." He shrugged lightly. "But I'm still out there looking for the right woman."

"Not me?"

"Certainly not you, Ally." He smiled. "The way I hear it, you're moving on to bigger and better things. Hollywood calls."

"I think I'll pass on Hollywood," she said.

He appeared to ignore that as just so much talk. "Can

they afford to lose you?'' he asked suavely, breaking off as the waiter approached.

Ally sat back while Rafe ordered, nodding her head when he suggested a particular wine. ''I've had another card from Brod and Rebecca,'' she told him more neutrally after the waiter had gone. ''That's four up to date. A phone call from their hotel in Venice.''

''I can claim a letter.'' Rafe's handsome mouth relaxed into a smile. ''Brod could very easily miss me if he rang. He made it sound as though married life is very well worth the risk.''

Her green eyes glittered. ''Do you have to sound so cynical?''

''*I* don't have any choice, Ally, darling, but I'm glad Brod has married the woman of his dreams. He deserves his happiness.''

Ally nodded her dark head, centre-parted, a mass of curls and waves. ''Marrying Rebecca was the best thing he could have done. She loves him with all her heart and of course she's very clever. Kimbara will be the perfect place to write. She told me she'd love to make a start on a novel. I'm sure she's got something in mind with an Outback setting.''

He seemed amused. ''Surely she got enough inspiration delving into the Kinross past. Sex and family secrets.''

''All right, all right.'' Ally waved an acknowledging hand. ''The Kinrosses never were as free of scandal as the Camerons. Anyway it's going to be a mystery thriller.''

''Great! I hope it's brilliant. I can even think up a title. 'The Disappearing Bride.'''

''The things we do to each other,'' Ally mourned. ''I used to be a part of your life.''

"Darling, you were part of *me*," he corrected, a sudden flare in his eyes. "You had it all. I know it was a long time ago, but let's get that straight." He was damned if he was going to tell her she had taken the life from him and left him a terrible emptiness in exchange. Obsession was a raging monster he had to conquer.

A great sadness came over Ally, a sense of having spoilt both their lives. "Now I'm your sparring partner."

He shrugged a wide shoulder. "It's better than being abandoned, believe me. Your kind of hold is tyrannical. There must be quite a lot of women with the underlying wish to own a man."

She stared at him out of her black-lashed green eyes. "I thought I could come back."

"You thought you could have an arrangement." His brows knit together. "Sorry, darling. I'm an all or nothing man. Obviously you can still affect me. I couldn't resist you the night of the wedding. I suppose I was off my head."

"Don't say that." She reached out urgently for his hand, wrapping her fingers around his.

She didn't see his knuckles whiten. "You use sex like a tool, Ally," he said, trying to harden his heart against the appeal in her beautiful eyes. "You're as near to being a dangerous woman as there is."

She sat back shocked, but not surprised. She wasn't wrong about Rafe Cameron. He had the pride of the devil. "I'm as needy as the next woman."

"Except the next woman doesn't have a fraction of your allure. Add to that, you're an actress." Mockery lit his sparkling eyes. "You've just gotta have that great response."

"Are you saying you've never slept with anyone who

offered better?'' Blood rose to her cheeks. She felt hot in her silk dress.

''Not in my experience. *So far.*'' He smiled at her, brittle, a little taunting. ''Even though something profoundly significant has been lost, we still share a powerful bond.''

''God, yes!'' Neither of them could deny it. Ally bowed her head, toying with her wineglass. ''That's very important to me, Rafe.''

''I know.'' He was consumed by the desire to take hold of her, crush her mouth under his. ''It's proof of the goddess syndrome. You let a man go on the condition he always returns.''

Midnight was breaking by the time they returned to Ally's apartment. Riding together in the back of the taxi had been an emotion-fraught experience made all the more tantalising knowing neither could have what their bodies so desperately craved.

There wasn't even a chance he would kiss her, Ally thought, deeply conscious of the languorous heat in her body, the flower of desire that was trembling for release.

Rafe paid the taxi off, joining her on the footpath and looking around.

''You shouldn't have let the taxi go. You mightn't get another.''

''Why are you whispering?'' he asked, taking her by the arm.

''I'm damned if I know.'' She could actually feel herself swaying uncertain of what was to happen next. She even felt guilty because she wanted him so badly, her whole body stirring in seduction.

Rafe kept her walking, taking time to check the dense foliage around the landscaped entrance. ''They really oughtn't let this get too high,'' he said, looking at a hedge. "I might have a word with the caretaker in the morning. Don't worry about me, Ally, I'll see you to your door. I'll be sure to pick up a roving cab. I could walk back to the hotel for that matter.''

Why not? He had abundant energy. He was a big, strong man. He knew how to defend himself against a charging bull. Lord he had taken on a half a dozen cattle duffers on his own, then went back to the muster.

The lift doors opened and they walked in, the small mirrored panels on the walls reflecting their images. She felt strung up. Ragged.

"Why do you look like that?'' he said under his breath.

She gave a little delicate shrug and put her hands to her flushed cheeks. "All I want is for you to love me.''

"*Make* love to you, don't you mean?'' All night he had been resisting the violent urge to touch her, now she was inches from him, staring at him with those emerald eyes. Her olive skin was flawless beneath the overhead lighting. Her short silk dress showed off her beautiful legs. The style left her arms bare but was cut high at the neck, covering her breasts. He knew exactly what they looked like beneath the black silk, the delicate curves, the points of her nipples. Did women know men regarded breasts as miracles?

"Rafe?'' she whispered low in her throat. A consummate actress playing a part? All he knew was he answered her with a soft growl, pulling her to him with one arm around her narrow waist.

Such an exquisite forbidden mouth!

"Rafe!''

"Don't bother talking,'' he muttered, given over to

consuming her mystery, though it was the source of his pain.

Her mouth opened fully to his exploration. He could feel the silk of her tongue, smaller, more pointed than his. She had closed her eyes, her head thrown back against his shoulder. He wanted to tear her clothes off, lay her beautiful body on a bed. His own body was filled with passion and agony, a great hurt having her in his arms couldn't block out.

He was dimly aware the lift had arrived at her floor. The door was opening. She was pressed against him, her arms going around his neck clinging as though without his support she would slip to the floor.

He drew them both out, walked a few steps along the corridor, before allowing his mouth to sink on hers once again. What she was offering might have been the elixir of life. Wall brackets were burning. No one was around though there were four units to each floor. He could feel her shuddering against him and his hand swept down over her breast uncaring. He remembered how it was those years ago. The first time in the big bedroom at Opal. She was frantic for him then. His little virgin.

She was frantic now.

Time to do something, Rafe thought, chiding himself bitterly but unable to think straight with Ally in his arms. He knew if Janet Massie weren't inside Ally's apartment he would have Ally on her own bed. Such passion for a woman was astonishing, bewildering. His mind said one thing while his body did a total turnabout. What he had often thought despairingly, was *exactly* right. Ally was in his blood. But he had to remember he had come here because she deeply needed his support and attention. There was something about that Harper character, though he tried hard to be affable, something quickly covered over like a blanket. To hide what? Psychological damage? It could well be severe.

Rafe's feelings of protectiveness released him. "You have to go inside now, Ally," he said, his voice changing from emotion-charged tones to the voice of authority.

"I don't want to go." She stared up at him, seeing the glow in his eyes, the passion that had emanated from him dissolving into a hard decision. "A pride of lions" is how people used to speak of the Camerons. Douglas Cameron and two sons. Rafe's hair was glinting beneath the lights as bright as an angel's.

Rafe saw the shadowy figure moving towards the stairwell before Ally. The figure seemed to be draped in some sort of dark cloak, still Rafe had the definite sense it was a man.

"Hey, you," he yelled on impulse. "Come back." His strong hands closed on Ally's shoulders, pushing her towards the door. "Get inside and stay there, Ally. And while you're at it, ring the police."

"No, Rafe!" Immediately she knew his suspicions. The figure had given off an unmistakably sinister aura. "He could have a weapon."

"If it's who I think it is I'll fight him with my bare hands." Rafe had learned many hard valuable lessons in life. One was how to defend himself no matter how rough the going.

He took off with no thought of his own safety, hearing the hard pad of footsteps on the internal stairway. With little more to go on than instinct he was convinced he wasn't far away from the man who'd been harassing Ally. The whole building was slumbering. There was no one on the stairs, no lifts opened and shut.

Just him and me, Rafe thought, hard in pursuit. Even

if he found he had the wrong quarry, the figure in the cloak had no business being inside the building. Whoever it was, it was no woman. This was a fit man equal to the chase. He tried to put a face on the fleeing figure. Came up with Matt Harper. It had to be him. He fitted the profile too well. Mead had confided as much glumly, unhappy they couldn't catch him out.

"He's probably writing up one of those letters now!"

This time, however, Harper had made a mistake.

The cloak, the surprise bit of apparel was thrown down early. Rafe leapt over it to the landing, with his long legs and his athleticism gaining on the quarry.

Three floors down it all came together. Rafe sprang in a rage, his anger made all the more formidable because it was deeply personal. He grasped the back of the man's neck and shook him like a rabbit, expecting violence, all that hate to detonate into an explosion of fists. Instead to his huge surprise, his quarry turned victim, shouting out a frantic, "Help!" He even ducked his head in his hands as though expecting to be beaten. Only Rafe had no killer instinct. He swung the man to face him, his whole demeanour incredibly tough and daunting.

"What the hell are you up to?" he demanded.

Matt Harper laughed shakily, rubbing his neck. "Jesus, are you cattle barons totally mad?" He laughed again, a choking sound.

"Pretty much so when someone tries to stalk our women," Rafe told him with contempt.

"*Your* woman, is she?" Harper gave Rafe a twisted smile. "You coulda hurt me, Mr. Cameron."

"I still can," Rafe warned. "What are you doing in Ally's apartment building and why did you run?"

"I did something stupid," Harper admitted. "But hell, man, I've got nuthin' to feel ashamed of. Since all this bad stuff has been goin' on I've been keeping an eye on Ally.''

"Yeah...sure.... Don't make me throw up.''

"Hey, mister, it's the truth!'' Harper straightened his handsome head, his expression proud. "It just so happens I care about Ally. She's the only one who has ever acted like a friend to me.''

Rafe nodded grimly. "Then it's a terrible way to repay her. You're as guilty as sin, Harper. I can see it in your face. I can smell the guilty sweat off your body. Anyway, for your information, I'm making a citizen's arrest. Ally has called the police. You can give your cock-and-bull story to them.''

Harper's black eyes flickered. "You won't come out of it too well, either, *Mr.* Cameron. There are laws against assault.''

"What's the betting you won't find anyone to look into it? I wanted to nail you, Harper, and I did. So now we walk. We're going back up the stairwell and you're going to wait quietly until the police arrive.''

"Oooh, you are a big strong man!'' Harper said, sliding into a simpering camp voice.

"Forget that!'' Rafe muttered in disgust. "That was just a smokescreen.'' He got hold of Matt Harper's arm and held it tightly behind his back. "Now start walking. I haven't hurt you but I'd like to. Remember that.''

They were almost at the first landing when Ally appeared at the top of the stairs. Her first reaction when she saw Harper was to cower against the wall. "Oh, God, Rafe,'' she moaned. "You were right, after all.''

At that Matt Harper's chiselled features contorted. "Right about what, Ally?'' he shouted, sobbing a little in perverse shame when he saw her beautiful stricken face. "I've done nuthin', I swear. Your big muscled boyfriend here has been belting into me. For what? For lookin' out for you. I've been doin' that since all that harassment stuff started."

"Go back upstairs, Ally," Rafe ordered, unimpressed with Harper's explanation, but Ally, being Ally, pressed forward unexpectedly, no longer fearful but violently outraged. Matt was lying. Of course he was lying, the miserable little rat. Why hadn't she recognised it? This was the person who had given her months of hell. Him with his black jeans, his black sweatshirt and that silly damned cloak.

"You bastard!" There were tears in her almond eyes. "And to think I stuck up for you. What a fool!"

"Go back, Ally," Rafe warned, knowing how impetuous Ally could be.

But she was focused on Harper. "You're going to pay for all you've done, Matt. I've rung the police."

"This is a set-up," Harper yelled, trying to stare her down, but Ally was flying down the stairs, badly shaken inside, but wanting to confront her tormentor. Those letters, those phone calls! She felt they had violated her. This repulsive creature needed a little time in jail.

"Ally!" Rafe yelled, rapid-fire as though she was about to step out into a mine field.

The tone of his voice checked her at the very moment her high heel caught in that damnable black cloak. She had a moment of pure panic, the realisation this was going to turn out badly, then she was pitching forward, throwing out her arms in desperation to break her certain fall.

This *can't* be happening! It was her last conscious thought.

Both men moved. Both cried out her name. Rafe felt he could have reached her, cushioned her fall with his body, only Harper, remorseful now, got in his way. Ally came down hard, her slender body at a sickening angle.

It chilled him to the bone. He literally had to heave Harper, who was howling like a pained animal, out of the way. "Move, you fool!"

"God, God, I'm sorry!" Useless words that made Rafe furious. He flung out a hand, crashed it down on Harper's shoulder, forcing him down on the step. Immediately his handsome features distorted. Harper began, of all things, whispering to himself, his head buried in his hands.

As Rafe bent over Ally, his mind slotting through all he knew about first aid, the door opening onto the stairwell burst open. Two men appeared, Mead and a uniformed police officer.

Rafe lifted his head, something dangerous in his face. "Get an ambulance quick. We have to get her to the hospital. She's had a fall."

The police officer acted on the instant, pulling out his mobile and punching in the emergency numbers.

"You got him?" Mead cried, his eyes on Harper who was screaming, to Mead's amazement, he hadn't done anything. They were trying to fix him with something he hadn't done.

"I got him," Rafe responded bleakly, working not to turn around and shut Harper up. Forcibly. Maybe for good. He kept hold of Ally's slender hand, his eyes glued to her white unconscious face. If anything bad happened to Ally, life as he knew it was over.

CHAPTER SEVEN

FEE entered the ward with great urgency, her face white and tense. She was followed closely by David Westbury, concern lines etched deeply into his forehead.

"Rafe, my dear!"

Rafe stood up as Ally's aunt went tearfully into his arms. "I've never been so shocked in my life. This is terrible, terrible. My beautiful Ally! Where is she? Where have they taken her?"

"They're running tests, Fee." Rafe tried to speak reassuringly, nodding over Fee's head to David who responded with his eyes. "She's broken her wrist. I don't know exactly *how* bad the break is. It's the crack on the head that's the greatest worry."

"My God, not head injuries." Fee's voice was frightened. "This could be very serious."

"I pray God not, Fee," Rafe responded, his hazel eyes grave. "Ally came to fairly quickly. She responded to my voice. She *knew* me though she was having a problem remembering what had happened. The paramedics were there almost immediately. She's having the best of care."

"We'll have to let Brod know." Fee looked terribly dejected. "On their honeymoon but they have to know."

"Yes, Fee," Rafe agreed. "I feel responsible for this somehow. My turning up seemed to have triggered Harper off."

"It certainly brought him out into the open," David

said supportively. The young man had nothing to reproach himself for. Rather the reverse.

"Rafe, dear, you can't blame yourself for anything." Fee shook her head. "We both know Ally. She wouldn't stand by idly if she thought you were in any danger. It's that psycho Harper we have to blame. Is he still denying he's had anything to do with it?"

Rafe nodded grimly. "His claim is he's been looking out for Ally, but the police aren't having that. He's been taken into custody and he'll be charged with being on private premises unlawfully, sending offensive material through the post, stalking, and there's the little matter of his violating privacy laws, ex-directory numbers and so forth. I expect he'll be released on bail with an order to appear in court a month or so on."

"Will Ally have to appear? She'll hate that." Fee shuddered.

"Not if he pleads guilty. If he doesn't she'll have to appear as a witness and be cross-examined by defence counsel. I don't think it will come to that, Fee. He'll be convicted and put on a good behaviour bond with a hefty fine. He'll also be ordered to stay away from Ally. I think it's something like a kilometre, so there goes his TV role."

"Who could care about that?" Fee's eyes shone with anger.

"Please," Rafe extended his arm, "why don't we all sit down. The doctors won't be back for some time."

A nurse with a kind capable face approached to ask them if they wanted tea or coffee, but all three declined.

Finally the doctor Rafe had spoken to earlier, a consultant neurologist, came down the corridor, his clever face expressionless in the manner of doctors, yet it turned the blood in Rafe's veins icy. He stood up to take the news while Fee, equally strained, clutched at David's arm. "Oh, Davey, I'm so afraid. I keep remembering Ally when she was a little thing and her mother had gone away."

David forced a smile, fighting down his own anxieties. "Ally's a strong girl, Fee. A fighter. She'll come through."

Rafe introduced Fee and David, and the doctor began to fill them in. The scaphoid bone in Ally's left wrist had been broken but he didn't foresee a problem with that. She was young, she was healthy. No reason to believe she wouldn't knit well. The head trauma? Well.... The doctor went on to explain Ally had a good strong bony skull which protected the tissues of the brain. Also she was fortunate in her abundant hair which unquestionably had cushioned her fall. Nevertheless, she had a split to the scalp that had required urgent attention.

He was awaiting the results of the MRI, the magnetic resonance imaging, which would provide him with all the information he wanted. He needed to know what was going on inside the cerebrum though he told them pools of cerebrospinal fluid acted as an internal shock absorber. The patient was badly concussed, but there was no significant impairment of physical function apart from the broken wrist. She had a very bad headache, as could be expected, but so far, and this was crucial, no visual deficits.

Her short-term memory however was at this stage poor. She would have to be held for observation. Perhaps for several days. The implications of any head injury had to be regarded seriously. He was at this stage reasonably predicting a quick recovery. There was no coma. The paramedics had reported the patient had recovered consciousness by the time they arrived, a matter of minutes.

"Can we see her?" Fee asked, standing up suddenly as though she wouldn't brook any other answer.

The doctor hesitated a moment, taking in her distress. "For a very short time."

"I only want to kiss her." Fee stared back into the doctor's eyes.

Immediately he turned, beckoning to a nursing sister who was standing at a station nearby. "Sister Richards will take you."

"Thank you so much, Doctor." Fee looked at David, who had no thoughts of intruding.

Feeling a shade dizzy with relief, the two men sat down as Fee and the nurse moved off. The doctor looked down at Rafe with a sympathetic eye. "Of course you may see your friend for a moment, Mr. Cameron." Obviously they were romantically involved. The young man was deeply troubled.

"Actually I'd like to stay through the rest of the night," Rafe said, hoping the doctor wouldn't argue.

"You don't have to." He was assured. "The hospital will call if there's anything worrying to report."

"I'll stay all the same."

The doctor nodded. "Very well. I'll have my pictures then. If you're still around I can give you a first-hand report." He began to excuse himself. "Now I have another patient I must see to. When your aunt comes back, Sister will escort you to Miss Kinross's room."

"Rather better than we thought?" David said after the doctor had gone, looking at Rafe with kindly eyes.

"I can't relax until she's been given the all clear," Rafe answered, unconsciously twisting his strong hands. "This has been a nightmare."

"But a major breakthrough, Rafe. Ally is very fortunate you were around. They should really lock Harper up and throw away the key. One tries to make allowances for his deprived background, but he sounds a piece of goods.''

Rafe nodded. ''He's got a lot of psychological baggage. I'm putting my hopes on the DNA. Mead tells me he's got himself a good lawyer already. That doesn't make any of us particularly happy. The police or me.''

''Ah, here comes Fee,'' David murmured, looking down the silent corridor. ''Is it my imagination of does she look twice as fragile.''

''Shock,'' Rafe said. ''She and Ally are very close.''

Closer in a way than Fee and Francesca, David thought, but didn't have the heart to mention.

Fee was deeply upset by it all, so both men encouraged her to return home.

''I'm staying for the rest of the night, Fee,'' Rafe told her. ''With any luck they might allow me to sit quietly in her room.''

''This has been a horrible shock,'' Fee said. ''She knew me but she couldn't really talk to me.'' Fee went to Rafe, hugged him. ''Thank you, Rafe, dear. The break is in the same arm she broke as a child, you know.''

''When she was ten.'' Rafe easily cast his mind back to the day. Ally the tomboy had followed them, him and Brod, out to their new secret swimming hole about three miles northwest of Kimbara homestead. It was a wonderful spot, a fair-sized lagoon with sparkling volumes of water pouring over giant boulders and swirling down a narrow gorge of multicoloured rocks with stripes of desert red, pink, yellow and black.

They were having a wonderful time in the water, surprisingly deep and cold, but both of them were fine divers and swimmers when suddenly the ten-year-old Ally appeared out of nowhere. Even as a kid she'd been a great tracker. She'd waved to them from the top of the rocks, tall for her age, in her T-shirt and jeans, her wildly unruly dark hair decorated with a garland of white daisies.

"Hey, you two! As soon as I get my clothes off, I'm coming in."

Both he and Brod had reacted with alacrity. That was all right when they were small and she was hardly more than a baby but not now. He and Brod were fifteen years old, nearly men, and both of them held Ally very dear to their hearts.

Immediately Brod had turned for the bank, starting to protest when Ally took off like a bird, her small feet flying among the stones. She probably would have made it to the creek only a sulphur-crested cockatoo chose that very moment to fly shrieking into the branches of a white-boled limewood that flanked the stream. He fancied he could still hear her sweet piercing cry, a cry resembling the cry she had made tonight.

They'd fixed her up with a stout stick along her arm, tied with his bandanna, carrying her all the way home on a makeshift stretcher they'd rigged up, leaving the horses, including Ally's, to find their own way home. Nearly fainting with the pain, Ally had been very brave. Even when all three of them had had to face Stewart Kinross.

No mother like his own to fly out onto the verandah filled with loving concern for her child, Kinross had given them all a tongue-lashing. Ally included. Rafe always thought Kinross would have liked to give his son a hiding but at fifteen both he and Brod had stood a boyish but extremely fit six feet. Brod and Ally had found little comfort in their father whereas he and Grant had had immense love and respect for theirs.

Now, when he was shown into Ally's hospital room, his heart literally sank in his breast. She was lying back in the bed, her left forearm in a cast, her normally vivid face robbed of every vestige of colour, her beautiful green eyes dull and heavily lidded. She didn't look remotely like a young woman in her mid-twenties. She looked little more than the child he had known and loved. A felled child after one of her famous escapades. Her wild silky hair was scraped back from her face and she had a surgical dressing over the left side to the back of her head.

Yet she tried to smile at him, her voice barely above a whisper. "Could have been worse!"

A standard joke between them when things had gone wrong.

"Ally." He approached the bed, bending to touch his lips to her temple. "My poor little Ally."

"You used to love me, didn't you?" she said, glancing down at her injured wrist. "Would you believe it, it's the same arm I broke all those years ago when you and Brod had to carry me home on a stretcher."

"I remember." He turned a tender, twisted smile on her.

She stared back at him almost dreamily. "I remember how you stood up to Dad when he started to yell at us. He really wanted to knock Brod flat, you know."

"He was under a strain," Rafe said it for the Sister's benefit.

"No he wasn't," Ally protested.

"Don't let's worry about it now, Ally." He tried to soothe her agitation.

"I've got a lovely big gash on my head," she told him hoarsely. "They had to put a dozen stitches in. And they cut out a patch of my hair."

"No one's going to notice, Ally. You've got lots of it." The old sweetness hovered around his sculptured mouth.

"Rafe." She tried to swallow down her panic. "I've no real idea what's happened. You've got to tell me. Fee didn't get an opportunity. They hurried her out so quickly."

"She was told she could only stay a minute, Ally."

She looked very haughty, eyes flashing. "Lovely to see you, too."

"Here, now." He took hold of her free hand. "We can talk all about it in the morning. By then you'll remember for yourself."

"That's right, dear," Sister intervened. "You've had an unpleasant experience. Doctor wants you to rest quietly."

Ally lifted her head, winced. "Rafe, here, will take full responsibility," she said. "He's used to lots of responsibility. He's Cameron from Opal. The Chosen One."

"Now there's a vital piece of information." Rafe bit back a laugh. "Do you remember we had dinner?" he asked. He drew up a chair to the bedside.

Ally frowned, concentrating hard. A movement of the brows that appeared to give her pain. "I remember we had dinner. I remember the two of us in the lift, then it starts to get hairy."

"The very reason why I think we should wait to talk about it in the morning. I'll stick around. The doctor said I could."

"Stay here." Ally began to grumble as he started to get up. "They couldn't give me much in the way of pain-killers. Not with concussion. I want you *here*."

"I think not, dear." Sister sailed in, an authority figure.

"I'm the patient," Ally pointed out, for all the world like Fee in one of her imperious moods. "And I say I want him here." She appeared to grow angry.

"Right you are," Sister agreed cheerfully, nodding her head at Rafe. "If you can sit down a little way from the bed, sir."

"I want him *right* here." Ally waved Rafe back. "I'm a must-go-where-he-goes sort of person."

Rafe had no idea why she said it. This was Ally, who had left him.

It was Rafe's first experience of a night in hospital. How the patients were supposed to sleep with all the light and noise he couldn't imagine. Nurses made regular checks on Ally, lifting her eyelids, checking her pupils, noting things on her chart, smiled kindly on him. In the dawn light before she was even stirring he was told to leave. Someone, he found out later a woman doctor, gave him coffee and a couple of muffins she'd been actually saving for herself. He went to the washroom, saw his own face in the mirror, weariness and worry apparent in his eyes and as he ran an explorative hand over his face felt his jaw with its golden stubble. He powerfully needed a bit of good news.

He got it as he was coming back from putting a call through to Fee. David had answered the phone. David who was fast becoming a fixture in Fee's life. Fee had been unable to sleep for hours, David told him. Finally she had dropped off in an armchair about six o'clock. As for himself, like Rafe, he had spent a long sleepless night. Stress was affecting them all.

When the neurologist told Rafe there was nothing in Ally's tests to cause worry, he fully understood what gratitude was. A tremendous sense of relief spread through him, as though a great burden had been lifted from his shoulders. He marched right back to the phone and put through another call to Fee's home. This time Fee answered in an uncharacteristically tiny voice that totally changed when Rafe gave her the good news.

"Oh, thank you, God," she cried, her resonant tones vibrating down the wires. "I've been so afraid. As a family we've been rocked by tragedy. You, too, Rafe, darling. I know Ally loves you."

Rafe put down the phone, shaking his head. Yes, Ally loved him in her fashion. Neither of them would ever forget their shared childhood, or their beautiful, romantic bonding, but inevitably after Ally got her strength and confidence back she would return to her career and the proposed movie despite her claim she wouldn't take up the opportunity. At least this time there wouldn't be a Matt Harper on the scene. Even if that tiny curl of hair didn't come from Harper's body, he'd have a hard time keeping to his trumped-up story.

"I want to go home," Ally told him the minute he saw her. "I'm perfectly all right. I remember everything." She did look a little better, eyes brighter, but nervy, obviously still traumatised.

"That's wonderful," he said with relief, "but you'll have to be patient, Ally, you're here for a few days."

"I'm leaving this afternoon." She was enunciating too clearly, moving her uninjured hand up and down on the coverlet. "I hope you can help me, Rafe. You're my pal, my protector."

"That I am," he agreed quietly, saddened and angry this had to happen to her. "But think about it, girl. Your doctors want to keep an eye on you. They're the experts.

Not you or me. It makes good sense to do what you're told.''

"I suppose," she said. "I'm just being stupid. Remember how I was always getting into trouble when I was a child?" The expression in her eyes softened. "Ally the daredevil, always trying to be one of the boys.''

"Yes, darling, I do.'' Her sheer vulnerability and her physical weakness were bringing back all the old powerful urges to shield and protect her.

"Thank you for still calling me darling.'' She rested a trembly hand over his.

"That's quite all right, kiddo.'' He yielded to the impulse to lift her hand and kiss it.

"You know I idolised you and Brod,'' she said with sweet recall. "You were both big brothers to me then. The two of you so famous for your bushcraft, the wonderful way you had with a horse. Fee used to call you The Twins though your colouring is like day and night. You the golden boy, Brod with his raven hair.''

"You always trying to tag along.'' He smiled as memories began tumbling over one another.

"You mustn't have wanted me all the time but neither of you ever got annoyed. I used to love your visits. I used to love going over to Opal.'' Her eyes started to sparkle. "Your parents were so kind to us, the motherless Kinross kids. Your mother always made a point of kissing me good-night on our stay-overs, sending me home with some beautiful little gift. She was a lovely, lovely person. I think of her so often.''

Rafe could feel a harsh throbbing in his own chest. "She certainly loved you,'' he told her, his tone suddenly clipped. "The little girl she never had.''

Both of them were quiet for a time, then Ally said,

"She really believed we were going to get married one day."

She hadn't lived to see the break-up.

"Ah, well, Ally, we blew it," he said steadily, his gold-flecked eyes cool as a rock pool. "But I'm still in your corner when anything goes wrong."

She felt his withdrawal. Saw it in his eyes. "I recognise that, Rafe, and I thank you for it." Ally looked down thoughtfully at the cast on her forearm. "I was lucky, wasn't I?"

"Lord, yes." He raised a hand to his temple. "It makes me ill just thinking what could have happened. You're so damned impetuous. Even as a child, you seemed to have no regard for life or limb."

"Excuse me," she said with some affront. "It was *you* I was worried about. I thought he might have a weapon."

"No weapon," Rafe responded tersely. "That will work in his favour. God knows what he came for. I didn't think he meant to confront you. I think he wanted to discover what you and I are to each other."

Her badly bruised body still reacted, filled with glittering spirals of heat. "Well, he got a damned good idea. All that frantic kissing!"

Though his heart twisted at the memory, he managed to speak lazily. "It's not as though we plan to do it again."

"At least until I'm out of plaster." Ally slumped back against the pillow. "Oh, that black sweatshirt." She shuddered as it all swam back to her. "The look in his eyes. Like a dog apologising for giving you a good bite. What I wanted to do was give him a piece of my mind."

He couldn't help smiling, his iridescent eyes crinkling at the corners. "I told you, Ally Kinross, you're a dangerous woman. By the way, I sent a fax to the Cipriani in Venice. Brod and Rebecca weren't there when I rang so I faxed the message to ring me or Fee. I explained a bit. Not much. I didn't want to alarm them at that stage. Now, the Lord be praised, we'll have better news when they ring in.''

"I don't want them to come home." Ally spoke emphatically.

"They might have other ideas." Rafe knew how much Brod loved his sister, and Rebecca was pretty fond of her, too.

"Not on their honeymoon," Ally maintained. "I'm not going to ruin their lovely time together. I'll convince them I'm quite all right."

"Don't get uptight." Rafe soothed her. "I happen to agree, but you'll need help when you go home. Janet, I'm sure, will stay on."

"You've spoken to her, of course."

He nodded. "She sends her love. Like the rest of us, she was terribly upset."

"Poor old Janet, she's had too many upsets. It's not the apartment I want to go back to, Rafe. I want to go *home*.''

"To Kimbara?"

She lifted her face to him and looked straight into his soul. "The place where I was born. The place I love with all my heart. The place my father kept me from."

Rafe winced with the memory of so much heartbreak. "He wasn't much of a father, was he?"

Ally sighed deeply. "He simply didn't have the qualities that went with the job." Of a sudden, her lovely voice became muffled. "Oh, Rafe," she murmured. "I'm so afraid."

"Of what?" He leaned towards her. "It's not your nature to be afraid."

Weak tears welled in her eyes, tears dashed impatiently away. "I'm afraid Matt will talk himself out of this. He can be very convincing. God, he even convinced me he was my friend. I just couldn't stand it if he was around. I'd rather quit the show."

His heart sank at the thought of her resuming her career, but of course she would. "So go home for a while, Ally," he advised. "We'll take care of you. It's only natural for you to feel this anxiety, but hang in there. Even if the hair that was caught on the Sellotape is something else, a fibre of some kind, I know the police will break his story. Innocent people don't run. They don't act unlawfully. They don't dress up in ridiculous cloaks. Of everything, that's what gets to me. It's so damned bizarre."

"Maybe he fancied himself as Batman." Ally tried to joke. "But he's ruined it all for me. I can understand now how that TV presenter, Gillian Craig, got out of the business."

"Being harassed would make anyone extremely nervous. One crucial thing, though, he didn't lay a hand on you. This is in the hands of the police now, Ally. Concentrate on your future." He spoke gently, trying to calm her, though his heart was heavy. "A very bright future if all the critics are to be believed. I'm sure you'll get to make your movie yet."

CHAPTER EIGHT

A FAMILIAR landmark was coming up. Manarulla, a vast naked rock of ever-changing colours that dominated the approach to Opal Downs' southwestern border. Ally felt excitement beat inside her like wings. Like all the rocks of the inland, Manarulla put on a daily pageant of changing colours. From a distance it rose from the vast red plains in a blue sea of mirage that turned an astonishing violet before the atmospheric haze disappeared as they flew through it. Looking down she could see all the horizontal bandings of raw earth colours that signified Manarulla's tremendous age.

At the start of the good season the endless plains were thickly vegetated with soaring river gums and ghost gums along the countless watercourses, the spreading billabongs and the chain of lagoons that dominated the Channel Country landscape. Even the arid mulga scrub showed off varying greens, the stunted branches, sculptural in their stark, outflung arms. While the pungent spinifex with its tall seed-bearing spears was so thick across the fiery earth from the air it resembled scorched fields of grain. These same mulga plains that ran on to the horizon within a few weeks of good rains turned into the greatest garden on earth, with an astonishing palette of colours. No one who had seen them could ever forget Nature's fantasy.

Beyond Opal lay Kimbara. Home. The Kinross desert fortress lay further towards the great living desert, with its rolling red dunes, salt lakes and shimmering gibber plains of polished quartz. She was thrilled to be back. Thrilled! So intense was her love for the land. As a child she had gloried in the daring deeds of her ancestors, the Outback's legendary heroes. The Kinrosses and the Camerons had covered themselves with distinction, their families interconnected down through the generations.

More important she was coming home to *peace*. Much as she grieved for what might have been, the fact her father no longer reigned over Kimbara gave her release. No more being hurt. No more baffling black moods to contend with. No deep regrets, no frustration for lack of understanding and communication. No futile craving for affection. Her father had been such a complicated man.

Her brother, Brod, was a man of a very different character, like their grandfather, Sir Andrew, Fee's beloved Sir Andy. Brod loved her and wanted her. Her sister-in-law, Rebecca, was blessed with a tender nature.

Now they were in clear sight of Opal's runway with its huge silver hangars emblazoned with the station's name on the roof. Three Cessnas were on the ground. A distance away was part of the helimuster fleet. Ally counted four in number, maybe the yellow tip of one positioned in one of the hangars.

"How many helicopters has Grant got now?" she asked, full of admiration.

"Six," Rafe said with satisfaction. "My kid brother is a very shrewd businessman and he's a great pilot. He has eight on the payroll now. Three other pilots, all experienced older men, a couple of top bush mechanics, maintenance men, office people. He's doing very well. Better than we both anticipated."

"That's the Cameron name. That counts for a lot."

"Sure, but Grant is *young* to have such big ideas.

Young to run a company that's getting bigger every day.''

''He's full of confidence. Like you.'' Ally smiled. ''I'm certain he's going to be a big achiever.''

Rafe nodded, a smile around his handsome mouth. ''He has visions of starting up his own airline.''

''Qantas eat your heart out!'' Ally laughed. ''What's he going to do when he gets married?'' She meant, where was he going to live? Was he going to continue to operate from Opal? Was he going to build his own home on the station? He was bound to find a suitable spot in five million acres.

Rafe shook his head. ''I'd like him to stay single for a while longer.''

''Drat it, you can't live his life for him, big brother.''

''I'd like to give him a fighting chance at any rate.'' Rafe turned his head to give her a quelling glance. ''He needs time to work up the business.''

''The right wife could help him.'' Ally was enjoying teasing him.

''The right wife, of course, is the lovely Francesca, your cousin.''

''Might I remind you, Francesca is a country woman.''

''Take another look down there, Ally,'' he urged. ''It's beautiful, it's savage, it's immense. It's unique. It's *empty* except for a handful of people, the great herds and the native fauna. It has absolutely nothing in common with the tranquil green beauty of England with its constant rainfall. This is the sun-scorched land where it mightn't rain for years. You love it. I love it. We were born to it. We're part of the desert scene. Francesca is a beautiful young woman. Warm, friendly, intelligent, but an exclusive creature. I'd be very careful if you're trying to promote a romance.''

"Promote a romance indeed!" Ally chuffed. "Grant has always been greatly taken with Francesca. The same goes for her."

"It's not *her* kind of life, Ally," Rafe warned.

"Might I remind you our ancestors hailed from the misty Isles. Now their bones have become part of the desert sand.''

"God, Ally, you're a matchmaker," he groaned.

"Maybe I am."

"Except you're not set on marriage yourself." A sardonic glance.

"I could be."

"Is hubby going to stay at home while you're off making movies?" he asked suavely.

"I haven't committed myself to anything, Rafe," she frowned, realizing it was an uphill battle convincing him she spoke the truth.

"You will." He said it casually, like he didn't care any more.

"Are you sure you don't want to land on Opal?" she asked a moment later.

He shook his head. "No, I'll get you home. You'll want to rest. You won't want to start up again. You can come over to Opal anytime you like."

"Don't think I won't take you up on that," she said.

It was a magnificent clear and cloudless day. Rafe turned downwind in preparation for the descent. There was Kimbara homestead, a jewel of colonial architecture set down in the ruggedly majestic wilderness, the main compound surrounded by its outbuildings like a small town. Kimbara was a self-sufficient community with its overseer, stockmen, ringers, jackeroos, fencers, mechanics, cooks and gardeners. There was even a small school-house with a resident school teacher for the children of employees. Even during the hard times, Kimbara hadn't suffered much in the way of cutbacks, thanks to the excellent management of the cattle chain and the family fortune.

The sparkle off Barella Creek that meandered through the home gardens was almost blinding as was the glinting corrugated iron roof of the hangar with Kimbara Station painted in huge black letters picked out with cobalt blue.

She felt ecstatic! Safer in the vast empty bush than she had ever felt in the nation's largest city. Of course her experience with Matt Harper had coloured her perceptions and robbed her of some of her natural resilience. So, too, her injuries which might curtail her normal station activities. Ally was a fearless rider. She had grown up adoring the companionship of horses. Now she wondered how best to go about station life with her forearm in a cast. Driving, too. How well would she handle the jeep? She had no intention of sitting around twiddling her thumbs. The wild bush called with its solitude and wonder.

Rafe turned sharply over the homestead, dipping his wing to signal to Ted Holland, Kimbara's overseer, they had arrived, then they were coming in to land, making a perfect touchdown despite the brisk cross-winds.

Ted was waiting, with his wife, Cheryl, who had opened up the homestead and stocked the refrigerator in preparation for Ally's arrival. In Brod's absence Kimbara's housekeeper was off visiting her sister in New Zealand, so Ally would have the homestead to herself. Something she wanted. Fee and David planned on arriving the following week. Fee had wanted to come at once but Ally had persuaded her she needed a little time on her own. She wanted to *think* in this other world of her childhood, in the freedom and immensity of the ancient land, without the city's jarring discords. She needed to compose herself in mind and body.

While Rafe stood in discussion with Kimbara's overseer, Cheryl accompanied Ally into the house which smelt of flowers and furniture polish. Cheryl had placed a huge bowl of brilliantly coloured zinnias on the library table in the front hall and Ally stopped to stroke a scarlet petal. All the time she half expected her father to stride out; tall, muscular, strong, in his riding clothes, always slapping at his side with his riding whip, extraordinarily impressive. *Alive.* Ready to pick an argument on the slightest provocation.

"Thank you, Cheryl. The flowers are a lovely touch," she said, genuinely appreciative.

"I'd do anything to make things nice for you, Ally. You know that. Brod took time off to send us a card." Cheryl smiled, obviously happy about it. "Venice looks wonderful. Another world. We were so pleased to get it. They're having a lovely time."

Ally nodded. "I had a hard job convincing them not to come home," Ally told her wryly. "They were really shocked by what happened to me."

"You and Brod are so close. It must be really scary being in the public eye." Cheryl, who rarely left Kimbara station said in a kind of awestruck tone. "Rafe told Ted the young fellow who's been harassing you has changed his tune."

Rafe came up behind them, his tall figure silhouetted by brilliant sunshine. "Guilty," he said with satisfaction. "Once he knew he'd left a little calling card, he folded.

The police will let us know when the case comes before the court but Ally doesn't have to go.''

"Well, it was a dreadful thing to happen.'' Cheryl looked dismayed at the cast on Ally's forearm. "Not that you haven't done damage to that arm before. Now...'' She started to bustle towards the rear of the house with them following her up, a small wry woman with a cap of salt and pepper curls, snapping dark eyes and a network of fine lines etched into her face. "I made a lovely cake first thing this morning. You'll love it, Rafe, men have such a sweet tooth, and a batch of biscuits. You can have them with your cup of tea. I'm happy to make it for you,'' she offered.

"That's all right, Cheryl.'' They moved into the huge, shining kitchen and Ally patted Cheryl's shoulder. "I'm not an invalid and I don't want to put you out. It's a comfort to know you're around if I get into any trouble, but mercifully it's my left hand.''

"Don't try to be too independent, dear,'' Cheryl warned her. "Don't forget I've known you all your life.''

"Are you saying I misbehaved?''

"You're telling me.'' Cheryl clicked her tongue. "Wasn't it Rafe here who christened you the naughtiest little girl in the world.''

Ally smiled sadly. "Most of the time I was trying to get my father's attention.''

In the end Rafe made coffee for them both, slicing a couple of thick slices of Cheryl's delicious cherry and ginger cake.

"Let's have it on the verandah,'' Ally suggested. "I want to breathe in our wonderful air.''

"You're not a bit daunted at the prospect of staying here on your own?'' Rafe asked when they were comfortably settled. He wasn't too happy about it himself but Ally was very stubborn.

Ally shook her head, her mass of curls piled untidily but very fetchingly on top of her head. "This is my home, Rafe, it might be full of ghosts. I'm sure I've seen little Mary Louise Kinross playing in the garden even if she did die at age six over a century ago. Kimbara's ghosts and I understand one another."

Rafe sighed in agreement. God knows his own heart jumped around Opal. "I know what you mean. But it so happens, I'm talking about your managing with that hand out of action."

"Give me a little credit, darling." She spoke briskly. "I'm Ally, remember?"

He gave her a very attractive lopsided grin. "You have to be feeling a little emotional to call me darling."

"You're kidding me." Ally shrugged, setting her cup down. "I've called you darling a million times."

His expression was frankly mocking. "Strange, I haven't heard it since you were a teenager."

"When I thought you had an excellent memory, Rafe?"

"You mean the night of Brod's wedding," he retorted smartly, "it was never too clear what you were saying."

"You're not curious?" she asked, trying to sound casual, leaning back in the white peacock chair.

"Too damned scared to be curious," he drawled. "I remember the last spell you laid on me."

"Now you're too proud." A stray ray of sunlight was making a glory of his thick golden hair, gilding the fine modelling of his face with its distinctive cleft chin. She took great pleasure in the shaping of his wide shoulders, the hard muscles of his arms and chest. He was a wonderful-looking man. The same tough Outback stock as herself. She began to feel her emotions churning and it showed in her eyes.

"Don't try to pick a fight with me, Ally," he warned lazily, watching the breeze further tousle her hair. She was wearing a pink cotton shirt and a matching full skirt. Clothes she must have found easy to get into. He couldn't help noticing through the unbuttoned neckline she wasn't wearing a bra. A problem with the cast on her wrist. Again it was there. The quick rush of desire, the waves of urgency that made him want to sweep her into his arms. They had been so companionable these last few days, but he knew how easy it was to get swept into the rapids. "Let's have a pleasant time," he now murmured. "We might take a walk later if you're up to it. I'd like to have a look around."

"That would be nice." *Nice?* When being here with Rafe was some way to a miracle. Ally turned her head, looking towards Kimbara's historic home gardens. Five acres in all. She could see three cowboy-gardeners going about the never-ending job of maintenance. It was a wonderful view from the wide verandah; great stands of native gums, tea-trees and palms, sweeping lawns kept green with bore water, a million blue and white summer-flowering agapanthus, the same huge semicircle of hydrangeas given welcome protection from the big heat by the trees. There were hundreds of flowerbeds, providing brilliant splashes of colour, a formal rose garden to the rear of the house with pergola bush roses everywhere, the sparkle and sound of running water, meandering Barella Creek with its flotilla of black swans and a small colony of ducks, its clumps of bullrushes, arum lilies and other water plants like the wonderful tropical blue lotus.

With all the nectar-yielding shrubs in the grounds it was a garden of birds. They filled the dry aromatic air with their songs and whistles, the flash of their brilliant plumage. As a child she had run around the garden imitating the bird calls, delighting in confusing them so they actually answered back. She had been a wonderful mimic. Still was for that matter.

Rafe was following her gaze, soaking up the garden's beauty and tranquillity. "Every time I come here I mourn what's happened to Opal's garden," he said. "It sorely misses my mother's presence. I detail some of the men but they're no gardeners. They just know how to clean up."

"You need a woman, Rafe," she said gently. "You need a wife."

I want you back, he thought with a harsh throb of pain. Instead he nodded. "I'll have to give it serious thought. I've let things drift so long. Ours was one hell of an emotional entanglement, Ally. I can understand sometimes how you had to flee from it."

"Can you?" She turned her head to stare at him with her green eyes.

Underneath he was still a touch hostile. "It frightened you as much as it gave you excitement. We always had easy communication. Sex just turned our world topsy-turvy."

Her glance wavered. "I never wanted to leave you, Rafe. I never wanted to make you unhappy. Making people unhappy isn't part of my nature. You had such strength, such maturity beside you I guess I felt like a wild kid out of school. I was the chosen one. I had the greatest joy and pride of being your choice for a bride."

He carefully suppressed the old anger. "Ally, darling, you weren't a shy awkward kid," he drawled, "you weren't any quiet little virgin blushing when a man sought you out. You weren't a young woman just beginning to explore your sexuality. You were born knowing the lot! I didn't seduce little ole you. You were dead set on getting us *both* into bed.''

She laughed mirthlessly, unable to deny it. ''You can say that again. You were everything in the world I wanted. I couldn't wait to know your body. God knows I'd admired it often enough. I thought I had it all figured out.''

''Then you got swept up by something else. The big career. You were always full of wild enthusiasms. Marrying Rafe and settling down on the farm didn't seem like such a good idea, after all.''

''You hurt me as much as I hurt you.'' She turned her face to him.

''Lovers usually do. Anyway we're older and wiser now, Ally. Unloved. Unattached.'' He was simply teasing but she reacted sharply.

''Don't make it sound like it's all too late!''

''No, there's always Lainie,'' he said in deliberate provocation. ''Now there's a girl with a lot of colour in her cheeks. A healthy girl with a good womanly body.''

''A good breeder?'' she asked ironically.

''A man needs children, Ally.'' Abruptly he sobered. ''They provide us with an excellent reason for living, for striving. I like to think my genes are immortal.''

''Well, you'd better get a move on, then,'' she answered tartly, unable to catch herself.

''All I need is your blessing, Ally. Now,'' he sidetracked. ''Don't be surprised if Lainie decides to call on you. All that business with Harper hit the papers. She's bound to want to call. She's a very sweet girl.''

An hour or more later when Rafe was leaving she made him take Cheryl's cake and her homemade biscuits. No cake-makers on Opal. No live-in girlfriend. No wives.

"Wouldn't you rather keep it?" he asked as she went about putting the biscuits in tins, crisp cookies in one, raspberry coconut slices in the other.

"No, these will be a treat for you and Grant. I love cake but I don't eat a lot of it. I have to watch my figure."

"What figure?"

It was just a little joke but some deep ache quickened. She turned abruptly away.

"Ally?" He couldn't imagine that he had hurt her. His beautiful Ally.

She shook her head but he could see her face screwed up fiercely just like when she was a kid and fighting the desire to cry.

"Ally, I didn't mean anything at all." His hand gently cupped her shoulder, turned her to him. "You've got a beautiful figure. It's just that you're really too thin."

"Oh, to hell with my figure!" she burst out, knowing she sounded foolish. "Do I have to beg you to kiss me goodbye, Rafe Cameron?"

"Ah, Ally, what can I say." Violent longing shook him but he bent his head intending to peck hr cheek then fly off home, only she moved. He couldn't endure not kissing her any longer. Her injuries had quickly gutted his sense of self-preservation. She was always in his heart. Day and night.

He moved his mouth gently but strongly over hers, finding it waiting, open, as sweet as the fruit from the tree of knowledge. He tried to keep the high level of sensuality down to a manageable level, but it swirled around them like licks of flame. She was standing very quietly, not moving at all, allowing him to kiss her, to slide his hand through the open neckline of her shirt, another button coming loose as his hand claimed the warm ivory silk of her breast. He could feel that wonderful sexual energy crackling between them, wrapping them in coils of gold. Ally, intensely aroused as ever by his ministrations, the highly sensitive nipples of her breasts drawing into dusky peaks as sweet as berries. She was so perfectly shaped for loving. His loving. He took profound pleasure in her.

She was moaning a little, delighting in sensation, he the expert on her body, the sound rising, circling like a singing bird freed from its cage. It extended his desire, making it terribly hard to retreat. He could feel the tremble in his arms starting, a sure sign passion was eating him up.

Rafe threw back his head, full of sudden, explosive frustration. "If I don't get out of this damned kitchen..." Ally was the only woman in the world capable of doing this to him. It was enraging, humbling. And yet...

"Maybe we should undergo counselling," Ally suggested wryly, her voice reflecting her own struggle. She was so hungry for him. In so much need. Being apart had been terrible.

"Maybe we oughtn't be alone together," he grated.

She gasped at the implications. "Don't say that! It's horrible. I want to come over to Opal. I haven't seen it for so long."

"Did you really expect to?" He cast a stern eye over her beautiful, flushed face. Deep as his voice was, it rang. "I wanted marriage. You rejected the whole idea."

"But, Rafe," she pleaded, laying her head against his chest, grateful beyond words when his arms automatically enfolded her. "I want to come."

"Then how can I possibly deny you." His smile was

grim. Ally, the consummate temptress. Every part of her he knew intimately, her satiny flesh. The scent of her skin. Her flavour. Would it ever work out or would they always be coming at each other through barriers. "One thing, my on and off lover," he warned. "You're not *sleeping* over."

She knew just what he meant, her body sparkling with relief. "Would I with Grant in the house?" she joked.

It was his turn to laugh. He had to. "Ally, you'd dream up a way," he said dryly. "You'd even risk breaking your bones."

For two days Ally roamed the station in the jeep. From cool early morning when the sky was tinged with indigo and yellow to the glorious sunsets that set the sky on fire. There was simply no other place on earth that filled her with such a sense of peace, of belonging, of ancestry. Remote it might be, frighteningly lonely to some, she saw beauty everywhere. Desert, dunes and plain, the ancient eroded hills and the hidden valleys, that magic of the caves with their extraordinary rock paintings, the endless chains of billabongs that were a major breeding ground for nomadic waterbirds.

Her favourite birds were the ones that didn't migrate, the sulphur-crested cockatoos, and white corellas, the galahs and the brilliant parrots; the zillions of small birds: the crimson chats and the wrens, the finch and the quail, the great flights of budgerigar flying in formation over the plains, literally turning the sky overhead to emerald with flashes of gold.

It troubled her to see scores of pretty little zebra finch feeding on the ground only to have a hawk leisurely swoop on the group. The falcons and the great wedge-tailed eagles liked to take their prey on the wing. That was nature. She had never become so thick-skinned that she didn't hate the kill.

At first, Ted, feeling responsible, was dead against her taking the jeep out, although she promised she would drive slowly to allay his fears.

"What if you go over a damned pothole?" Ted said. "What if you run into a bloody camel? They're ill-tempered beasts at the best of times. There are two big males on heat out in the hills. We came on them only the other day, fighting each other and roaring with rage."

"You didn't shoot them?" Ally well knew the wild camels, descendants of animals imported into the desert in the early days of settlement did a great deal of damage, particularly to fences.

Ted shook his head. "We try to tolerate them. But they're a worse nuisance than the donkeys."

"I'll keep to all the recognised tracks," she promised, full of zeal to oblige.

"You'll have to, Ally." Ted twisted his battered akubra round and round in his hands. "Rafe would tear strips off me if you had an accident."

"So who's going to tell him, then?" Ally asked with insouciance. "Anyway, I haven't done anything stupid for years. I've been driving around the station since I was twelve. I'll have no difficulty controlling the jeep. Besides, when has a broken arm or a broken leg for that matter stopped you?"

Ted scratched his balding head. "That's all very well, Ally. I'm a tough old bird."

"So am I." She laughed. "Don't feel bad, pardner. Your concern is charming."

And she was true to her promise. She took care, keeping to the main tracks and limiting her speed. Once a

kangaroo leapt out from behind a boulder to stop dead
on the track right in front of her, staring at her in the
familiar dopey, endearing, fashion as if she could possibly do anything to harm him. Ally obliged by going
around the big marsupial. She visited the mustering
camps, watched a couple of fine-looking brumbies being
broken in by Barney Crow, their part aboriginal stock-
man who had a wonderful way with horses.

The men at first were a little shy of her, even the ones
who had known her all her life. She wasn't one of them
any more. She was Miss Kinross who had gone away to
become famous. It didn't take Ally long to make the
awkwardness disappear as she enjoyed a cuppa and a
slice of damper baked over the hot coals with them during a break.

Ally had always found it easy to make friends. Her
father would have been coldly disapproving. He was one
of the old school who kept himself many, many steps
removed from the station staff. Ted Holland was the only
one who had ever been allowed into the homestead. And
then only to give an accounting.

Her nights were unsettled, the old fears clawing at her
dreams. It would take her a while to recover from her
trauma, but by day she was always on the move, causing
Cheryl to remark on her energy.

"I would have thought your nasty experience would
have made you want to relax, Ally," she called from the
verandah of the Holland's comfortable white timber-
framed bungalow.

"I am relaxing, Cheryl," Ally answered her. "I adore
being home. My biggest fear here is having an emu or
a kangaroo jump at me."

The house was enormous after her apartment. In the
evenings she turned cupboards out. Had a look inside.

She found lots of photographs of herself when she was very small. Many of them when she was a baby. She never realised she was so cute. Even then she had a mop of curls. She couldn't imagine her father had taken them. It had to be her mother or Grandpa Andy.

Her mother! Even the word was an elegy. *Mother.* Was it possible her own relationship with Rafe had been influenced by her parents' disastrous marriage? When it got right down to it, at that point, she was so *young,* she had feared marriage. There had been such an overload of emotion. All her childhood and early adolescence there had been a near mystical bond between herself and Rafe. The relationship that had been definitely nonsexual, more like family, overnight culminated in Rafe's becoming her fantasy lover.

All those hormonal upsurges! She blushed to think of them, the powerful needs and the crazy wishes. In its way growing up had been a traumatic experience for her. She had fallen wildly in love too early when love meant: *pain. Her mother going away.* Her mother had been passionately in love with her father at the time of their marriage, but in the end she'd been forced into leaving him. Maybe in fleeing Rafe she had been trying to protect herself against such a bleak eventuality.

Except Rafe was an entirely different being from her father. As a woman who had been intent on mastering a career, she recognised that fully. Even if Rafe had slammed a door on her. Rafe wasn't into control and dominance that masked a fragile ego. Rafe wanted a wife as his life's partner, with the full security of his support and love. She thought establishing herself as an actress was a worthwhile goal. Now she found she didn't want that at all. The Dream was still the same. The Dream was Rafe.

CHAPTER NINE

ON THE third morning she heard the most welcome sound in the world. The sound of Rafe's Piper circling the house. Now at long last she would get to see over Opal, the historic homestead she had once expected to go to as a bride. The homestead where she had fully expected to live out her days as Alison Kinross Cameron. Both sides had fully supported that once. Even her father who had related far better to Rafe than he ever had to his own son. Why that was, she had ceased to wonder. Perhaps it was because Rafe was a Cameron, a different dynasty. Brod was the Kinross heir who for years had performed the real tasks of running the chain. It was Brod, like Rafe, who had the true dedication.

She was waiting for him at the airstrip when he landed, leaving the jeep parked in the shade of the trees. Within minutes they were airborne, Ally filled with anticipation for what the day might bring.

"Should I bring my nightie and a toothbrush?" She tried a joke when he rang to invite her over, wanting to behave perfectly but finding herself too darned nervous to manage it.

"Whyever would you need to do that?" he'd answered suavely. "I'll have you home before sunset."

"You used to invite me for the night," she'd reminded him with some nostalgia, trying desperately to get back on the old easy footing.

"Sorry, Ally, darling, you're banned for life."

So that was that! Nevertheless she'd tucked a too'

brush into her tote bag in the wry hope he might relent. She realised she was all but flinging herself at him, but her pride seemed to have flown out the door.

Her first sight of Opal's homestead brought a flood of memories surging back. Rafe's mother had always been up there on the verandah awaiting their arrival. A warm friendly woman but always maintaining her dignity. They had been great friends. She so needy for motherly attention, the older woman with a household of men, touchingly appreciative of young female company.

"What are you thinking about?" Rafe asked, almost reading her mind.

"How your mother was always waiting for you on the verandah."

The dull pain never went away. "How you and she used to talk. Chatter, chatter, chatter. Even Dad had to ask you to put it on hold." Delighted to see them both laughing and happy.

"We women had tons of important things to discuss. Fashion and gossip. Novels we had read. Who was getting married. Who was breaking up. Families who were in trouble and what could be done to help. What was going on in the rest of the world. We talked about everything. Your mother loved to hear what Fee was up to. I think she got a lot of vicarious pleasure out of Fee's glamorous life without ever wanting to lead it."

Rafe smiled. "I know. We used to tease her. Obviously two husbands aren't enough for Fee?" He gave Ally an amused sidelong glance. "David has settled in very nicely."

ld only nod in agreement. "I think he's always
h on Fee. Not that he didn't love his wife."
ving to pair them off?"
ans a lot to me," Ally said. "I think she and

David could be very happy together. David is a very cultured man of wide interests. Fee's at a time of life when she's ready to settle down.''

"I'm strangely moved by that.''

Rafe's mouth curved in the way she loved.

"But it wouldn't go down too well with Francesca's father, would it?'' he asked.

"Mmmmm.'' Ally took time to consider. "He could hardly object. He and Fee were divorced years and years ago. The earl has happily remarried.''

"But why pick his *cousin*?'' Rafe raised a questioning brow.

"David is the best man, that's why. Don't be a spoil-sport, Rafe Cameron.''

"I'm sorry,'' he apologised, a decided glint in his gold-flecked green eyes. "I adore your fabulous aunt. She provided us all with a lot of colour.''

The 4WD swept around the circular drive, gravel crunching under its heavy tyres, Rafe bringing it to a halt at the base of the short flight of stone steps that led to the verandah.

Opal Downs homestead, a single-story structure, lacked the conscious splendour of the two-storied Kimbara built in the style of a grand English country mansion, and its home gardens, as Rafe had warned her, had suffered badly, but Ally loved it probably because the homestead had soaked up all the love and devotion that had gone on within its walls. It had a palpable aura of serenity and comfort.

The house was a fine example of English Regency adapted to suit the harsh Outback conditions. Wide verandahs surrounded the house on three sides, protecting the central core. The timber balustrades, the fretwork and the classic pillars were all painted a pristine white, the series of timber shutters at the French doors a dark glossy green, lending a charming airiness and sense of coolness to the house.

The main structure was composed of a particularly fine rose-coloured brick that had mellowed to a graceful desert pink. The slate roof added another touch of elegance, the green toning harmonising with the all-over colour scheme. Like Kimbara, constructed at the same time, a wealth of skills in the way of tradesmen had been borrowed from around the colony, builders, woodworkers, plasterers, stonemasons. Charles Cameron and Ewan Kinross had been in competition to see who could complete their homestead first.

Charles Cameron, less concerned with grandeur had finished many months before. Ewan Kinross marked the completion of his splendid gentleman's residence by taking to it a bride, Cecilia, his kinswoman, whom both men loved. Rebecca, as Brod's bride, would get to wear Cecilia's famous opal and diamond necklace now. Indeed Rebecca had already worn it to a ball, drawing a great deal of attention to herself as her father had intended. Just to think of the old story, Ally found upsetting, so she pushed it away. Brod and Rebecca were married now with a long happy life in front of them.

"Let's make a ceremony of it, shall we?" Rafe asked as he helped her alight from the Toyota.

She tipped her face to him, her eyes challenging. "You're not going to carry me over the threshold?"

"I doubt I could stand the weight."

"I thought you were the one who kept telling me I was stick thin." She let go of his hand, breathing in deeply to cover a whole range of emotions. "It's such a beautiful day I suppose Grant is up and away?"

He nodded. "Pretty close, as it happens. Victoria Springs."

"What?" she stared at him hard. "I really hope he doesn't tell Lainie I'm here."

"Should that put a dampener on anything?" he enquired very suavely.

"Don't be nasty, Rafe. So what form is this celebration going to take? I'm always open to suggestions." She shook her curly head tied at the nape with a silk scarf.

"Now isn't that a fact! Actually I put out a brand-new doormat in your honour. It says Welcome."

"But *am* I?"

"I don't know. You wouldn't have been up until recently." The remark came out a lot more crisply than he intended but it was intensely unsettling having her back on his home ground. Having her back where they had first made love together. He could still feel the enormous wound to his pride, to his psyche, when she had gone off and left him. Sure the wound had healed over, but the place still plagued him like a phantom limb.

Going to bed with Ally was as inevitable as taking his last breath. That hadn't changed, but he wanted no more deep confusion in his life. She would return to her career and her large network of friends within the business. He would have to accept what couldn't be changed and find himself a satisfactory wife. There were any number of beautiful, desirable, intelligent women out there. Let's face it, he figured on the Most Eligible list. He'd find a good wife if it killed him.

"So are you deciding this was a bad idea?" Ally confronted him in her spirited fashion, in her own way extremely proud.

He shook his gleaming golden head, a certain measure

of wry resignation in his voice. "Opal welcomes you back, Alison Kinross. I guess your spirit will never leave."

"No, it won't!" Her green eyes glittered like emeralds. She turned to him so quickly, her sable-sheened hair whipped around her face. "I laid a claim to you, Rafe Cameron, when I was a child. I love you better than anybody. Better than anyone else will. You just remember that." She swallowed convulsively on the emotion that rose to her throat.

He studied her with a taut smile on his mouth. "Make sure to remind me at my wedding. Much as I love you, Ally, I can't go through life with your hooks in me."

"Hooks?" Ally winced involuntarily. "You really don't want me back?"

His heart lunged, though he spoke satirically. "Are you ready to toss your career aside?" he countered, taking hold of her hand and leading her to the steps. "I don't think so, Ally. It makes me awfully sad, but that's life."

She spoke what was uppermost on her mind. "You know it scares me sometimes the way everyone believes I'm going to follow in Fee's footsteps."

He froze. "Hell, Ally, isn't that what you've been working for all this time?"

"I have no pretensions to stardom," she said as emphatically as she could.

"You could have fooled me." He was mocking now, holding her hand on the verandah.

"I guess I have," she agreed quietly. "I thought I wanted to prove I could act. Or prove I could be somebody out there in another world. I suppose I wanted a *choice*."

His mouth twisted ironically. "Yes, you did, and you

made one. You've put in a lot of hard work and it has paid off. I'm not into watching much television, as miraculous as it's been for the bush, but I've watched your show and I have to say you're something special. You're beautiful, you're spirited, you radiate warmth and intelligence. You're delightful. The camera loves you, the way you walk and talk, the radiant flash of your smile, the bubbly laugh. You have an individuality about you, a glow. I'm not in the least surprised the movie offers are starting to come in.''

She went to the balustrade and slid her uninjured arm around a white pillar. ''Everyone is very disappointed I'm leaving the show. They're planning on killing me off while I'm out on some errand of mercy. Needless to say, Matt has buried his career.''

''I'm not surprised.'' Rafe's voice was a rasp. ''He's barely civilised. Do you have to go back to finish some scenes?''

''No.'' She paused to watch an eagle in flight. ''They're working on it. I'm still having nightmares. I'm even hesitating before I pick up the phone.''

He joined her at the rail and placed his hands lightly on her shoulders. ''It'll pass. Give yourself a little time to regain the harmony in your life, Ally. You're strong. You'll find yourself again.''

His attitude plainly warned her he gave no serious credence to any talk of her abandoning her career.

He let her wander around the main rooms of the homestead at her leisure.

To the left and right of the spacious hallway graced by arches, flowed the old drawing room and the formal dining room with their matching richly carved fireplaces and mirrored overmantels. The beautiful ceilings with their detailed plaster work had unquestionably been done by the same team of craftsmen who had worked on Kimbara, with very fine crystal chandeliers adding their own elegance and splendour. The formal dining room led to the library through wide folding doors with pedimented overdoors that almost reached the sixteen-foot-high ceiling, beyond that the huge study Rafe had taken over from his father, and a smaller one on the other side of the passageway used by Grant.

The mainly Victorian furnishings with a selection of rather splendid Oriental artefacts were still in an excellent state of preservation, but Ally itched to replace a lot of the soft furnishing as Rafe's mother had planned to do.

Virtually nothing was changed since the last time she had been in the homestead. It was fairly obvious, too, the brothers, Rafe and Grant, kept almost exclusively to the less formal rooms of the house, using the morning room, which adjoined the huge old kitchen, for meals and the large informal sitting room facing the rear garden and a loop of the creek, to relax.

While she was exploring Rafe stood quietly watching her circle each room in turn. If she hadn't been an actress she could have been a dancer, he thought. Her movements were so graceful, so fluid, so springy. He remembered all the dances and balls they had attended together. Outback people revelled in such occasions.

The balls on Kimbara had been marvellous. Stewart Kinross had been very much the lord of the manor with his wonderful good looks and his dark glinting sardonic manner. Ally had a high look of her father, as did Brod, except for his startling blue eyes, but when you saw Ally you automatically thought of the brilliant Fee. It must have broken Sir Andrew's heart when his adored daughter left her Outback home to set sail for England, Rafe thought.

Fee's father, Ally's grandfather, had loved his only daughter deeply. Fee's spreading her wings had stopped all his plans. Of course, Sir Andrew wanted her to marry someone like his own father and settle down to life on the land. Sir Andy had wanted grandchildren. Lots of them. He had three, it was true. Two he'd adored so openly, and little Francesca, born last, almost inaccessible to him, shielded by her father's English family.

It was very quiet in the old ballroom, which hadn't been used in many years. The Kinrosses had built their great hall to accommodate cattlemen's conferences and their gala functions; the Cameron dances had always been held here with homage paid to their Scottish ancestry, an ancestry the Kinrosses shared as did many Outback families.

Ally stopped in front of a magnificent portrait of Charles Cameron in full Scottish regalia that hung in the ballroom above little gilded settees and chairs that were pushed back against the walls. A few feet away was a companion portrait of his wife, with the Cameron tartan arranged with great panache around her bare shoulders and her billowing white silk ballgown. Another Scot. She was smiling, a lovely-looking woman with a generous figure, reddish gold hair, large hazel eyes and high colour in her cheeks. Smiling radiantly no matter she had been married on the rebound after Ewan Kinross had wedded the legendary Cecilia.

"I wonder what went wrong between our ancestors," Ally paused to ask. There were any number of theories, but no one ever knew and the main characters had never said. "I can't imagine marrying one man when I was in love with another."

He looked at her, masking a flash of pain. "People make accommodations all the time, Ally. The girl I marry mightn't be *you* but I'm damned sure I can learn to love her."

"You can transfer your affections that easily?" She swung her head, fixing him with her eyes.

He nodded calmly. "I'm not going to doom myself to the bachelor life. I want family. Children. I love children. You should see me with my godchildren."

Whatever had she done walking away from this fabulous man. "I know you'll make a wonderful father." Ally moved further along to stare up at the portrait of Charles Cameron's wife. "This is where that wonderful flamboyant hair comes from. And the gold-flecked hazel eyes. Grant's colouring is tawnier. You're pure gold." Ally sighed, looking up at the painted familiar eyes. "She looks a lovely, open, good-humoured woman. I really like her."

"Not Cecilia the temptress," he pointed out, very dryly.

"Cecilia was doomed to be very unhappy, but this woman wasn't."

He gave a faint grimace. "I expect, like me, my ancestor reasoned the best way to go was get on with life. The marriage turned out to be long, happy and fruitful."

"I'm glad." Ally turned about, giving him her incandescent smile. "You Camerons are such nice people. My grandfather had hopes Fee and your father would fall in love."

"Yes, I know. I don't feel bad it turned out differently. Dad admitted once he had a crush on her. I might even go so far as to say everyone did, but he knew Fee wasn't going to settle down like a good Outback wife. Fee was going to fly the coop and never come back."

Even as he was speaking, Rafe felt the old traitorous twist of his heart. Like aunt, like niece.

"Dance with me?" Ally suddenly asked. "Let's pretend it's the old days. Didn't we have the mot wonderful times? I remember as a child staring into this room, watching all the grown-ups dancing." She closed her eyes and began to sway around the room. She was sick to death of the cast on her arm. She couldn't wait to get rid of it. "Isn't it romantic, da da da da da." She couldn't really think of the words, on a night like this.... "Isn't it romantic."

Around and around she went in a loose summer dress, sleeveless, low in the neck, the fine, white cotton printed with one huge yellow hibiscus across the skirt. A little girl's dress, except Ally wasn't a little girl. She was all woman. With the cast she was forced to keep one arm to her side but the other lifted as if to go around a partner's neck.

Everyone had wanted to dance with Ally. All the boys. Ally as light and drawing as a flame. She had a lovely clear singing voice to match her voice. Absolutely true, but she was making a mess of the lyrics. He had to stop himself from joining in. He wanted *her* to stop. He wanted to prevent her from reclaiming his heart. But he wanted the taste of her lips on his tongue. He wanted to pick her up and carry her through to the silent master bedroom with its great four-poster bed. Memory of the first time he had taken her slid into his mind, an experience so profound he knew if he lived to be a very old man it would be one of his everlasting recollections.

"Dance with me, Rafe." She called to him. "Come on, please. Some memories never go away. I remember the way you looked at me when you saw me dressed for Corrie Gordon's twenty-first birthday ball."

And Ally was sixteen. Overnight turned from a tall, graceful, skinny, tomboy who used to pop up out of nowhere into the most alluring woman. How had it happened so fast? One day she was still caught up in the craze to go fishing for barramundi, the next she was wearing a dark green velvet dress with long tight sleeves, a low oval neckline that showed the sweet curve of her delicate breasts and a swaying bell of a skirt. Instead of riding boots, evening shoes with the glitter of diamanté adorned her feet, her customary untidy plait as thick as a rope transformed into a gleaming dark cloud of curls that framed her beautiful vivid face.

"My God, would you look at her!" Brod, at his shoulder, had cried, the brotherly pride vibrant in his voice. "If she isn't Aunt Fee all over again!"

Even then Brod's remark had struck at him forcibly like a cold fist, though he had buried the remark deep. Fiona Kinross had gone away when she was only a few years older than Ally.

Now Ally slowed up to face him. "You're not a bit of fun any more," she accused.

"I'm not into *dancing* any more."

"It's a bit early to give it up," she lightly mocked. "You were a wonderful dancer. Everyone used to stop to watch us. It's funny how big men can be so light on their feet. I expect in your middle years you'll stomp around like John Wayne." She lifted her curly head. "This one for me? Please, my Raphael. My angel."

"No man in his right mind should get so close to you, Ally," he said, feeling skeins of desire unravelling.

"Remember how I used to call you that? My angel. You with the golden hair and the golden skin and the dazzle of your eyes."

"Lay off, Ally," he said, his iridescent eyes flickering with deep buried hostility.

She arched her swan's neck and gave a great big sigh. "Hell, Rafe, you're not going to turn into a *frog*?"

His reaction was immediate. Fierce, a little savage. He threw out one arm and jerked her to him, holding her body very closely against him, his breath coming deep and harsh. "What *is* it you want?"

She strained back a little so she could stare into his taut, handsome face. "I want you to marry me." Now that she had said it, it almost stopped her breath.

"What?" His deep voice was a thunder. She could feel the force of his anger like it was *live*.

"I said, I want you to marry me." A sudden rush of tears glittered in her eyes.

He knew he was a heartbeat from losing it. Maybe less. "Do you actually *mean* it or is this some cruel joke?"

"Never." She shook her head. "I want you. I need. I love you."

"You mean you want to ruin me." He gave her a terrible look of contempt.

"How could I ever do that?" She tried to put every-thing she felt for him into her eyes.

"I couldn't stand your going away, Ally," he grated. "I couldn't stand it then. I couldn't stand it now. My wife has to be with me. I have to know she's there. I have to know she's someone who's going to want our children. Who's going to be *there* for them. Look how Fee wrecked lives. Your cousin Francesca had a miser-able childhood. I suppose to this day her husband doesn't feel free of her."

All of which was true, but Ally fought back. "Don't

transfer Fee's curse to me, Rafe. I am not Fiona Kinross, I'm Ally.''

''And you want me to take you back?'' he asked with hard incredulity.

''You're going to take me back,'' she flared with her own powerful temper.

Incredibly he laughed. ''You're right, Ally. I'm going to take you. You want me to make love to you, don't you? Like wild sex is going to heal everything?''

''Not *wild*,'' she said very gently, touching the tips of her fingers to his sculptured mouth. ''You have to be careful with me. I've got fading bruises all over my body. I have this forearm. I have a big scar buried in my hair.''

''You know all about seduction, don't you?'' He took her face between his hands, outlining her wide beautiful mouth with the tip of his tongue, deliberately teasing her when he could feel that rising, head-spinning, extravagant passion.

''I'm not ashamed of it,'' she said, her dreamily beautiful emerald eyes closed. It wasn't said in arrogance, or triumph, but a simple statement of fact. Yet it gave him the lash he needed.

''Well, it's not on, Ally.'' Very slowly he released her, gratified his voice sounded cool and ironic though it cost him a huge effort. ''You're as spellbinding as ever you were, but I'm older and wiser now. I still retain a handful of my marbles. I don't know what's the matter with you today. I suppose the ordeal that Harper put you through has made you a little afraid. Your injuries have slowed you down, but in another few weeks you'll be out of that cast. Your head will be properly healed and you'll be thinking about resuming life. Your real life, that is.''

All her blossoming hopes plummeted. Sure she hadn't thought it was going to be easy. "So what do I have to do to prove I'm on the level?"

He looked down his straight nose at her. "I don't know if you can, Ally," he said, trying to sound philosophic. "Maybe you are. Maybe you aren't. Who knows with a woman? Let alone your kind of woman. I tell you what…" He took her arm with great courtesy. "Why don't we leave the whole thing alone until you're feeling more like yourself? I was thinking we could have an early lunch then take the horses out. I've heard all about your exploits in the jeep, now I can find you a quiet hack, not the usual temperamental firecracker you go for, and ride to Pink Lady creek. It's literally covered with the most dazzling waterlilies. You'll like that."

"Thanks, Rafe," she said quietly, knowing she was outmanoeuvred.

But not outmatched!

It was midafternoon. They were returning to the house after a ride of real companionship based on their mutual love of the land when they heard the sound of a chopper splitting the quiet air. It was apparent the chopper wasn't putting down at the airstrip, the sound was coming even closer.

"That'll be Grant," Rafe said, screening his eyes with his hand and looking skyward. "He's early, I didn't expect him until sundown."

"It will be nice to see him," Ally said with genuine affection. It would have been marvellous to spend the rest of the time alone together, but Ally had always been fond of Grant. "He's been mad about aircraft since he was a kid. Now he's made a thriving business out of it. I suppose you worry?" She knew he would. None of them after the Cameron fatalities had ever felt *really* safe.

"I try not to," Rafe sighed. "But it's not easy. Grant's all I've got."

"And me. And Brod." She glanced at him.

"And Lainie," he added slyly. "I expect you'll see her one of these days."

They saw her a lot sooner than expected. Grant set the helicopter down as lightly as a bird on the lawn while they watched from the verandah.

"He's got someone with him." Ally crinkled up her eyes against the brilliant sunlight. All hopes of having Rafe to herself were vanishing.

"I'm afraid so. Party's over."

The rotors slowed, then stopped. Grant was out on the grass helping his passenger to alight.

Lainie.

"Speak of the devil," Ally moaned.

"How can you say that of such a sweet girl? Smile, Ally, they're on their way."

"Howdy, you two!" Lainie yelled, and began to wave. "I cadged a ride with Grant."

"That's just awful!" Ally glanced wryly at Rafe. "Did Grant really have to tell her I was here?"

"Surely you want to have a word with one of your biggest fans?" he countered, amusement in his hazel eyes.

"I suppose I must," Ally sighed. "I don't know why I'm speaking like this. I like Lainie. There was a time we used to laugh ourselves silly."

"I take it you've sobered up?"

"Especially since she's taken a great interest in you," Ally told him tartly. "I expect you're the one she's really come to see."

"Let's find out." His face under the black akubra he still wore had a casual power.

Lainie and Grant made their way across the lawn to the front steps, Grant looking very much the action man in his khakis. Lainie dressed attractively in a rather fetching drawstring peasant blouse of many colours teamed up unexpectedly with tight designer jeans. Her thick fair hair, one of her greatest assets, flapped in the breeze as beautifully groomed as a show pony's mane.

"Ally, great to see you!" Lainie gave her infectious laugh. "As soon as Grant told me you were visiting I insisted he let me join in the fun." Her sparkling eyes moved to Rafe. "Why didn't you let me know, Rafe Cameron? Ally is one of my dearest friends."

"I would have, Lainie," he drawled, "only it took me ages to clean up the house."

Lainie leapt up onto the verandah, about to give Ally a big hug, stopping when she saw the cast on her forearm. "Oh, you poor thing! That's awful. We were all absolutely dismayed when we read what had happened to you in the papers. Mum said you made one big mistake when you left the bush."

Before Ally could react, Grant went to her and kissed her cheek. "Hi, Ally. It's true, we've all been anxious about you."

"And you've got so thin." Lainie's tone suggested Ally was visibly losing weight by the second. "That dress is hanging on you."

"That's what it's supposed to do, Lainie," Ally said. "I need things that are easy to put on."

"And end up with something very easy on the eye." Rafe's mouth curved in an appreciative smile.

"Thanks for that." She turned her head to him.

"Not really. I just loved looking at your bare legs when we were out riding."

Lainie wheezed abruptly, then started to cough. "You rode in that?"

"I've got nothing to hide. I tried but there's no way I can manoeuvre myself into jeans," Ally said. "I'll have to wait until the cast comes off."

"Yes, but…"

"Shut up, Lainie," Grant said calmly.

"I've had some news from Fran that might interest you, Grant." Ally briskly changed the subject. "She's quit her job."

"Blimey. I thought girls like her didn't need a job," Lainie interrupted. "Lady Francesca de Lyle. I thought Fran was just filling in time until she married a jolly old lord."

"So what is she going to do now?" Grant locked onto Ally's gaze, ignoring Lainie entirely.

"I think she wants to spend more time with her mother." Ally had the air of a woman who thought it a very good idea. "She can always get a job here."

Lainie fought to contain herself, failed. "It's all *your* fault, Grant. You were making goo-goo eyes at her at Brod's wedding. Leading her on," she teased.

"I was not!" he clipped off, bristling just a little. "Don't get my goat, Lainie, or I won't drop you back home."

"Only joking. Can't you take a joke?" Lainie punched him playfully on the arm. "I think Francesca is absolutely lovely and she *sounds* such a princess. I quite see why you were smitten."

"What about a coffee or a long cold drink?" Rafe smoothly intervened. "Are you going back right away, Grant?" He turned to his brother.

"I'll wait for Lainie," he said in an all-suffering voice. "Relax for a while. What else did Fran have to say?" he asked Ally as they all walked indoors. "More to the point, when is she thinking of coming?"

"I expect she's after him," Lainie confided to Rafe in a whispered aside. "Some of those old aristocratic families haven't got a razoo any more."

In the kitchen Lainie took over the making of the coffee with brisk efficiency, the men wandering off as soon as they saw she was handling it. "Aren't you a bit nervous over at Kimbara all on your own?" she asked Ally, going to *exactly* the right cupboard for coffee cups and saucers.

"I'm not on my own, Lainie." Ally stood over by the window, looking out. "There's Ted and Cheryl. All our people. Any one of them would come to my aid if necessary."

"I know. I meant on your own at the homestead." Lainie ground fresh coffee beans, continuing to talk over the noise. "Heavens, I could never manage to find my way around. It's so big."

"Not for me. So what have you been up to?" Ally asked, trying to divert Lainie without real hope of success.

"We've got a new dog, Kaiser," Lainie announced, looking pleased and proud. "He's magnificent."

"Don't tell me, a German shepherd."

Lainie laughed, selecting the largest plunger. "We love the breed. I know cattle dogs are more to your taste."

"Kimbara *is* a working station."

"So, when are you off again?" Lainie asked brightly, making heroic efforts to hide her jealousy.

"Give me time, Lainie," Ally pleaded wryly. "What's all this about?"

Lainie bit her lip. "You and Rafe are just friends. So you *said*?"

"So?"

"Gee, I don't appreciate having to ask you this, but have you any plans for staying over?" Lainie's fair, attractive face grew hot and ruddy.

"The things people ask you," Ally sighed. "Actually I packed my toothbrush."

"You didn't!" Lainie stared back at her horrified, glancing swiftly in the direction of the hallway as Rafe came back into the kitchen.

"Can I carry something out?" He couldn't fail to notice Lainie's open-mouthed expression. "What's up?"

Lainie felt so close to crying she couldn't hold back. "You've never asked *me* to stay over." She couldn't control her sudden hostility towards Ally.

"What do you mean?" Rafe looked from one young woman to the other.

"If Ally's staying, I'd like to stay, too," Lainie told him firmly. "We could make up a foursome and play cards."

"Are you crazy!"

"Now there's a mood booster," Rafe drawled. "The only snag is, Ally isn't staying over, Lainie. Neither are you. I've learned how to protect my reputation."

All anxiety left Lainie's face. "You tease, Ally," she said. "You and the toothbrush! You always like to kid around. I was just asking Ally how long she's going to stay with us, Rafe. When *are* you going back to Sydney, Ally?"

"When it's safe," Ally offered laconically.

"I can never work out if you're fooling or not,"

Lainie complained. "That wretched Harper. You'll have to make sure he stays away. Anyway, now you're going to be a famous movie star you'll be surrounded by security people. It's so exciting when you come to visit us. We envy you all your glamour."

She was jealous. Of course she was jealous, Ally thought, but she's making her point and, being Lainie, hammering it home.

"Where's that coffee?" Grant's voice called nearby. "I feel like I've been waiting for hours."

Lainie smiled brilliantly in Rafe's direction. A woman who could be relied on to be there. "Be right out!"

CHAPTER TEN

ALLY had Cheryl up to the house to help her prepare for Fee's and David's visit. They were arriving at the weekend, taking a domestic flight to the nearest Outback terminal where they would be picked up by Grant.

Bedrooms were opened up and aired, fresh linen fragrant with the scent of the native boronia, placed on the beds. Little welcoming touches were brought in, books, ornaments, the bathroom stocked with fresh fluffy towels, bath mats, washers, soaps, bath gels, toothpaste, hand creams, little luxury items. Cheryl went down the list, marking everything off. Fresh flowers would be placed in the rooms on the morning of arrival.

It was exciting to have members of the family at home, Cheryl thought, happily going about helping Ally. Brod and Rebecca, the new Mr. and Mrs. Kinross, would return home at the end of the month. Kimbara would blossom. Stewart Kinross hadn't used friendliness as a means of communication. His children did.

With a couple of hours of daylight left Ally decided to take the jeep out for a short run. She needed to think and the desert fringe was the place to do it. She'd received a long, newsy letter from Bart Morcombe, the director, with an accompanying script for a film the brilliant young New Zealand director, Ngaire Bell, was seeking to make. It was an adaptation of a fairly recent prize-winning Australian novel set in colonial times and offering a very challenging role for the female lead.

"This will take you right up the ladder of success,"

Bart had written. "Haven't I told you all along you've got the right stuff for a major actress?"

She wasn't the only actress Ngaire saw in the role but apparently the brilliant director had been very impressed when she spotted Ally in an episode of her country doctor series. "She loved your appearance and personality, Ally," Morcombe wrote. "The kind of passion you're able to generate. I really think you should forget the other project and concentrate on getting into Ngaire's film. I tell you it's a showcase role. And you being a Kinross from a landed family would have the background off to a T."

Ally read the script through in one sitting. She couldn't put it down. But strictly speaking, wasn't her interest professional, much in the way she would devour the performance of an acting icon like Dame Judy Dench or Katharine Hepburn. Where was her own drive to success? The absolute conviction she wanted to play this part, allowing Ngaire Bell would even settle on her for the lead. Surely she would snap up established stars. It was a risky business starring a relative unknown. But then it happened. Bart hadn't talked about budget, big or small. The film would be shot on location in and around Sydney before moving inland for the Outback scenes. No exact location as yet.

Ideas were buzzing in Ally's head as she headed out to the sand gravel flats. She had seen them so often smothered in wild flowers, "the white and golden glory of the daisy patterned plains," as some bush poet had put it. She only intended to run out a few miles to Moorak Hill, another monolithic red rock to the northwest. It was a spot that gave her great pleasure. A small stream, more a tranquil shallow billabong lay at its feet, a haven for waders and small birds who made their nests out of the large hollowed-out branches of fallen trees. Desert rivers and streams were marvellous places, their cool refreshing beauty providing such a contrast to the heat and red dust of the spinifex plains, such a huge part of the desert landscape.

Near the rust red eroded summit of Moorak with its small caves and series of small cliffs like a pyramid grew a beautiful ghost gum, its stark white trunk and bright green feathery crown standing out boldly against the glowing, opal blue sky. It had been growing proudly out of the sheer rock of the ancient bastion for as long as Ally could remember. A sight to fire the imagination.

When she reached her destination, Ally parked the jeep in the only protection she could find, a grove of gnarled little trees with precious few leaves to hide their extraordinary skeletons. It wouldn't be long before they succumbed to the arid conditions. Gnarled mulgas were a symbol of drought but good winter rains had fallen and better yet the far tropical north was expecting a rainy Christmas. When the monsoonal rains filled the great rivers of the north, life-giving water flooded down through an inland system to the Channel Country a thousand and more miles away. If the rains were really flooding they could reach to the very centre of the continent and into the vast basin of Lake Eyre, the largest salt lake on the continent, which filled maybe twice every century.

Ally reached out a hand to a leaf but it crumbled at her touch, releasing a strangely attractive scent, like dried herbs. Overhead coasted falcons and hawks forever on the lookout for prey. Ally reached back into the jeep and poured herself an iced coffee from the thermos. The big heat of midday was over, shadows were lengthening but the sun never lost its power. It was important never to become dehydrated. She drank slowly, revelling in her surroundings. The peace and quiet was extraordinary, like being inside an Outback cathedral.

How different it was being home. Home where she looked into the eyes of her beloved. This was where she grew up. This was what held her in place. She had seen enough of the outside world to know this was where she belonged. To know what was important to her. She had faced herself, confronted her needs. It came down to two choices. She could work hard and perhaps become famous in the career she had embarked upon or she could find her way back to being the only woman in Rafe's life. That might prove harder than winning a leading role in a Ngaire Bell film, she thought wryly. They'd had such a wonderful relationship. Beyond the physical. The spiritual, the emotional. She wanted that again. She wanted Rafe's full trust. She was ready in her mid-twenties to make a full commitment. To life. To family. She'd seen quite a few of her friends, fellow actors, women lawyers, busy P.R. consultants, career-oriented women becoming very reflective once they reached their thirties. There was a certain fear they might be going to miss out on their role as *women*. As wives and mothers. They knew they probably couldn't have it all like a man.

Nothing meant anything without Rafe. Ally's vision of herself as a highly successful career woman had burned out. She saw it very clearly now. Rebuilding her once marvellous relationship with him was her major priority. She was happy to forgo a career. It wasn't a very real sacrifice, either. It was her choice. Her way of settling the biggest issue of her life.

Feeling happier and more at peace, Ally returned to the jeep, turning it in a half circle before driving off through the tangle of cane grass. With the approaching sunset the smouldering blue of the sky was being invaded with billowing clouds of colour, rose, pink, amethyst and gold. Hundreds of birds flashed across the sky, going into the long smooth glides that landed them in the lignum swamps. Dawn and sunset in the Outback were magical times. Ally was watching a large squadron of brolgas flying in V formation just ahead of her when she became aware the jeep was overheating. Wisps of smoke were issuing from the bonnet. Her eyes flew to the temperature gauge. The needle was moving steadily into the danger zone. How could that be? She always checked the radiator for water. Number One rule. The jeep like all other station vehicles underwent routine checks.

"Oh, hell!" she muttered to herself, distracted enough to hit a fairly large half-hidden bough that flicked over and up into the air. A little awkwardly she climbed out, cursing her injured wrist, she managed to lift the bonnet without too much trouble then she began to make her inspection inside.

Damn! The radiator hose was coming away. She would have to tighten the clips holding it. Not much of a problem. A few minutes later she was on her way, realising she wouldn't reach home in daylight. Cheryl was bound to tell Ted when he came in. Both would be worried. Ted would most likely drive out to check if everything was all right. At least Cheryl knew where she was heading. She never left the homestead without leaving general directions. With her arm in a cast she had to be more careful than usual, more considerate of other people.

Ten minutes on with the burning red sun sinking towards the grape blue horizon she was forced to stop again. Not only had the hose come away again it was obvious the clips simply weren't going to hold it. The whole thing would have to be renewed.

"What now?" she asked the darkening bush. She wasn't frightened. There was nothing in the bush to hurt her. No wild animals, only innocent wild creatures. It grew cold at night, but she had a rug. She could throw it around her. There was a small bar of chocolate, a large red apple, the rest of the iced coffee. She could get a fire going. News she hadn't returned would travel fast. If they couldn't find her in the pitch black, blackness so acute it couldn't be imagined, someone would come for her at first light.

Ted saw the helicopter coming in, bright yellow with the Cameron logo an interlocking GC within a dark blue circle. He figured it had to be Grant calling in on his way home, probably to finalise dates for a Kimbara muster, but it turned out to be Rafe. He had the chopper set down before Ted reached the airstrip.

"Now this is a real surprise." Ted beamed, swinging out of his sturdy Nissan. "I thought it was Grant fixin' up for the muster."

The two men shook hands. "Grant's got his hands full right at the moment Ted, but he'll be contacting you soon. I was over at the McGrath place helping out with a problem when a new pile of mail came in. Quite a bit for Brod. Some of it I expect you can take care of. I collected ours and yours in advance. I'll say hello to Ally if you'll run me up to the house, then I'm off home. I prefer not to fly the chopper in the dark."

They found Cheryl waiting in an attitude of anxiety on the verandah of the homestead. "I expect it's nothing to worry about but Ally's not back yet," she called to them the minute they stepped out into the drive.

"So where did she go?" Rafe felt like swearing, his gaze checking the sky. Ally sure needed watching.

"She always tells me her plans." Immediately, Cheryl was on the defensive. "A few jobs needed doing this morning, Rafe, what with Miss Fiona arriving with her friend. Making up beds and such like. Ally likes to get out every day. She loves the sunset."

"So where did she say she was goin', luv?" Ted interrupted patiently.

"Northwest. Out Moorak way, I'd say. I'm just sitting here waiting for her to get home."

"Best go fetch her," said Ted, proceeding to turn back to the Nissan. "Why the hell Ally wants to rattle around in that jeep I don't know." He let out a great sigh. "I would definitely class Ally as a mighty independent woman."

Rafe made a quick decision, based on his intense involvement. "If you lend me the Nissan, Ted, I'll go check if she's on the way back. She wouldn't need to leave it too much longer or she'll be driving home in the dark."

"With one good arm," Ted said, clearly unhappy about that.

"The keys, Ted." Rafe held out his hand, not pushing his authority but it was instantly clear.

None of them dared think. Ally might have had an accident.

"Let me get some food in case you get stuck, Rafe," Cheryl called. "I won't be a minute."

"Fine." Rafe turned to Ted who obviously shared his concern. "I'll either see her coming in or she's had a breakdown of some kind. That's always on the cards. Either way I'll find her. If we don't make it back by nightfall you might give Grant a call. Explain what's happened. It won't be the first time we've spent a night in the bush. You might meet up with us first light.''

"Count on it, Rafe. I told Birdy to check the jeep." Ted sounded upset and worried. "Seein' Ally's always takin' it out.''

"She'd have trouble changing a tyre," Rafe responded a little grimly. "Don't worry, Ted. It's hardly your fault. I know how stubborn Ally can be. I'll find her." He looked a little impatiently towards the house as Cheryl came flying out carrying what looked like a picnic hamper.

"In case you need it," she called as Ted moved quickly to help her. "Food and drink. Won't hurt if Ally's on her way in.''

We should be so lucky, Rafe thought.

Thirty minutes out. No sight of her or the jeep. He had taken a rough track of sorts now he left it, the Nissan bouncing through tall yellow grass and over clumps of spinifex and fallen mulga. He was starting to concede they might have to organise an all-out search for her at dawn. Maybe she had run out of water? Maybe she was thirsty and headed for a creek? wouldn't make Moorak in the light. The sun was already sinking in a great fiery ball. Dusk would be short, a momentary amethyst veil, the vast red earth, the interlocking network of waterways, the crumbling hills, the entire landscape would be blocked out as night fell.

Unbidden but never far from his mind came all the old horror stories. This was killer country if you didn't know it. But Ally did. That gave him great hope. Ally wasn't likely to lose herself in the bush. She would stay by her vehicle even if she ran out of petrol or water or the vehicle broke down.

In the enveloping dusky light he could see the near pyramid form of Moorak. The best course at this point was to head towards it as quickly as common sense allowed. Again unbidden images of Ally. Face down on the red earth. Ally with her head wedged against the steering wheel, the bonnet of the jeep plunged into a crevice that had suddenly opened up for want of water. She wasn't strong enough yet to do the things she did. And yet, wasn't that the way of the bush where everyone was so active.

Stamping down hard on his panic, Rafe began to sound the Nissan's horn, the successive blasts almost painfully loud in the darkening desert. He would have to slow down. He could hit something, put his own vehicle at risk. At least Ally wouldn't be scared like a city woman would be. He'd seen tourists scared out of their wits after they'd been rescued from the waterless wilderness. With good reason.

A kilometre closer with the vehicle's headlights raying out across a night-time scene of aridity and desolation, contorted shrubs and gnarled branches like gigantic bonsai, he heard something.

"Ally!" The deep frown lines etched into his forehead evened out. That was the jeep's horn, answering him. "Keep it going, Ally." He dared to hope she was all right. "Slowly now," he told himself when he was desperate to let the engine rip. This was no smooth city road or even an Outback track full of potholes. This was the unrelenting wilderness. A dying desert oak reared up in the headlights, its twisted upflung branches giving the appearance of a nightmare scarecrow.

He swore beneath his breath, bounced round it, his ears tuned to the S.O.S. of the jeep. "I'm coming, Ally. Trust me. Everything is going to be fine."

But was it? Would the woman he loved with all his heart be forever out of reach. She had told him, in a weakened moment, she wanted to be back in his life. He seemed at that moment he would take her at any price. The Nissan bounced across the mulga plains, riding high across clumps of spinifex and tough twisted fallen branches then dipping sickeningly into narrow crevices and dry shallow gullies.

When Rafe finally caught sight of her she was standing in his headlights, her right arm supporting the injured arm with the cast. God, had she hurt herself? There appeared to be nothing wrong with the jeep.

"Ally?" he bellowed, tremendous waves of love and relief giving way to a crazy anger. Hell, she was even looking back at him like "Isn't this fun?"

It was no surprise then as he gathered her tightly into his arms she laughed aloud, filled with an irresistible happiness he had found her. "You'd better believe this, Rafe Cameron, I knew you'd come for me."

"Did you, now?" He couldn't possibly take it so casually. "I suppose you realise you've had us all terribly worried?"

Immediately she was apologetic. "I'm sorry. Truly sorry. But it's not my fault, Rafe." She pointed to the jeep. "The radiator hose went."

"What a damned nuisance," he muttered shortly. "Isn't Birdy in charge of maintenance?"

Ally flew to Birdy's defence. "Actually he did check it out." Now that Rafe was here, she felt like a kid at a party, no doubt helped along by that nip of brandy. "Isn't this super stuff?" she said blithely, deliberately echoing words she had used so often as a child. "We're going to have to spend a night in the bush together."

But Rafe's emotions were too close to the surface.

"What makes you think I won't attempt to drive back. I made it out here, didn't I?" He was aware he was somewhat curt.

"Indeed you did." She stroked his arm. "My hero. Don't be angry, Rafe," she begged him. "All's well that ends well. I'm not hurt. It was my first real chance to commune with the bush at night in years. Look, the stars are coming out." She lifted her curly head. "Millions and millions of them. You never see a sky like that in the city."

He clicked his tongue, looking around them. "We could do with a few streetlights all the same." They were standing in a very small pool of light given off by the Nissan's headlights.

"We are going to stay aren't we, Rafie?"

Her voice, such an instrument of pleasure was pitched low. She never called him Rafie except to tease and taunt. He understood that thoroughly. He looked down at her, seeing she was wearing a little denim shirt with short sleeves and a matching full skirt, buttoned down the front. She was wearing sneakers on her feet. "You're cold," he said suddenly, sounding angry. "You've got a rug in the jeep. You should have put it round you."

"I won't need the rug now. I've got you." She held his stare.

Abruptly he broke away, going to the jeep, and pulled the rug off the front seat. At least she had the sense to use it. "Here, Ally, this isn't funny. Put it on."

She did so immediately, her tone wry. "Aah, we're going to be businesslike, are we?"

"What were you expecting, a party?"

"A party would be marvellous." She stared back up at the blossoming stars. "A party for two. You haven't got any food with you by any chance? I'm starving. All I've had is an apple and a small piece of chocolate.''

"Well I can't say cutting back will do you any good. Yes, I've got food. Cheryl put it in. We'll have to make camp for the night. Were you going to stay here?''

Ally nodded. "I wasn't going to move until you came for me. I'm psychic where you're concerned.''

"Oh, yes, Ally, you've got all the answers,'' he groaned. "Get in the Nissan. I'll have to find a better camp site than this. You know damned well how the temperature falls at night.''

"So we're going to need to sleep together for body heat.''

Her hair fell in a dark cloud all around her face. Her green eyes glittered like a cat's caught in the light. "Full of fun, aren't you?''

She took his arm, hugged it, trying desperately to communicate her deep sincerity for all her covering banter. "Oh, I'm just so happy you're here, Rafe.''

"Good.'' He turned her gently but firmly. "Let's move. Think we can make it back to Moorak?''

"Sure.'' She walked with him to the Nissan.

"We might be able to find ourselves a small cave.''

"As long as you don't mind sharing it with half a dozen rock wallabies.''

"Not tonight.'' He helped her into the passenger seat. "Any wallaby that lives there will have to move on.''

They were moving slowing across the rugged terrain.

Ally started to laugh again. "I'm in such a good mood.''

"I can see that. Sure you haven't been getting into the medicinal brandy?'' he asked dryly.

A fresh bubble of laughter. "I did have a small nip to ward off the cold. I was born in the bush but I still can't get accustomed to the chill of the desert nights. It's so unexpected after the scorching days. What are you doing on Kimbara, anyway?''

"You mean you didn't divine the reason along with the fact I was coming? I collected a bit of mail at McGrath's. Brod's and ours. I decided to deliver it on the way home.''

"I hope you intended popping up to the house to see me?''

"I was going to pay you a visit, yes. No mail for you.''

"I got mine,'' she said.

"Who from?''

"Oh, Bart Morcombe.'' She spoke casually. "He sent a script.''

"Which you read?''

"In one long sitting. It's very good. There's a part for Fee if she's interested. Not big but it's important they get the casting right. Heck, what was that?'' she cried as the vehicle rocked on its side.

"A blasted boulder,'' he muttered. "It's a good thing we're nearly there.''

They set up camp beside the stream as Rafe couldn't find a suitable cave on the lower slopes. With great efficiency he went about making up the fire, then when it was burning brightly, he rigged a tarpaulin using stout boughs to make it act as a windbreak. Another smaller tarp served as a ground cover, over which went one of the rugs. Station vehicles always carried such equipment in case of emergencies and it worked well tonight.

"Now for the food,'' Ally said, on her knees busily setting out the contents of the old hamper she and Brod had used as children. "Let's see.'' She couldn't keep her hunger out of her voice. "Bread rolls.'' Ally delicately sniffed them. "Nice and fresh. Cheryl must have made them this afternoon. Lord, she's forgotten the butter. A block of cheese. Chicken, a chunk of ham, fruit. No bottle of wine. That's dreadful. We really needed a bottle of wine. And God bless her, nearly half a fruit cake."

"Sounds like a feast." Rafe grinned.

"We could toast the rolls. Burn them to crisp."

"No thanks, Ally. I'll take them as they come. I'm surprised you're so chirpy. I know you weren't lost, but it couldn't have been pleasant."

"I'm normally chirpy," she said. "Have you forgotten? Come and sit next to me. Come on." She grabbed his hand, pulled him down to join her on the rug. "Pretend we're kids again."

"Until you get some of your primitive urges," he said very dryly.

Ally gave a little snort of laughter. "When did you ever need encouragement?"

He ignored that. "So tell me about this new script you've been offered?" He accepted the ham and cheese roll she passed him, wrapped up in a paper towel.

"It's very good." Ally took a bite out of her roll, continuing to talk with her mouth full. "It's an adaptation of Bruce Templeton's novel, 'The Immigrant.'"

"I've read it." Rafe glanced at her clear profile gilded by the firelight. "I suppose you've been offered the role of Constance?"

She was so pleased he knew it. "No, I've been offered the chance to read the script, that's all. Apparently, Ngaire Bell, the New Zealand director, likes my work. Or likes *me*."

"Even I can see you in the part, Ally." He sat quietly.

"It might have been written for you, even to the physical description."

It was crystal clear to him now where Ally's future lay. Who was he to deny her the development of her gift? She wasn't any ordinary girl next door. She was immensely talented. She wasn't Lainie Rhodes who would make some Outback man an excellent wife. She was Ally. He might have known her since she was a small child, but Ally had something to offer the world. He loved her. He couldn't change it, only send her on her way. Marriage between them, and he was sure he could get her to marry him, would never work out. They would survive a few years. Maybe have a child, then the same old problems, distance, separation, would erode their love. He wouldn't want any child of his to suffer like little Francesca had.

"Would you like a drumstick?" Ally asked, so happy herself, she was unaware of his sombre thoughts.

"No, I don't think so," he forced a smile.

"Oh, come on! You're a great big man." She put the roast chicken into his hand. "I wish we had a bottle of wine."

"Me, too." All of a sudden he felt like getting drunk. A couple of glasses of wine wouldn't do it. All the alcohol in the world wouldn't numb the pain.

They finished with a piece of fruit each. Ally ate a mandarin, spitting out the seeds, Rafe settled for an apple. "Isn't this beautiful here," Ally said dreamily. "The air is so sweet and fresh we can do without the wine. I love the smell of the bush. It's absolutely unique. I love burning gum leaves. I love crinkling dried leaves into aromatic bundles. I love all the little sounds at night, bush creatures scampering around. I even love the distant call of a dingo. Such a mournful howl.'' She lay back and Rafe pushed a cushion beneath her head.

"My God, Ally,'' he said, looking down into her beautiful face, flushed in the coppery light.

"Why are you sounding so regretful?'' She lifted her hand, let her fingers explore the deep cleft in his chin.

"Regrets!'' He tossed his gilded head away from her like a high-mettled thoroughbred. "I have thousands of them. Haven't you?''

"Of course, I have,'' she retorted with some spirit. "One can't live without accumulating regrets along the way.''

"It's pointless to ask if you're going to accept the role if you're offered it?'' He rolled onto his elbow.

She stared up at him. "Even if I got the part I'd turn it down.''

"The hell you would,'' he said in a taut voice, looking down on her broodingly.

"It's very hard for me to get back your trust,'' she sighed, realising full well words weren't enough.

"It is that. I know you mean well, Ally, when we're alone together but don't you realise...''

"I realise I love you,'' she cut him off, her voice full of emotion. "I'll always love you. You built such strong defences they won't let you listen. But at some point, I beg you, you've got to believe me.''

"Well maybe I do, Ally,'' he sighed deeply. "Each of us stole the other's heart, but what happens if we marry? Do we bring a tragedy down on our heads.''

"Lie down beside me, Rafe,'' she begged. "Let me show you how much I love you.'' She fixed her light, sparkling eyes on him, full of entreaty.

His heart was pumping wildly. "No, let me show you,'' he rasped. Why was life such a mess? Why did love put one at such risk of losing? His arms came under her slender body warmed by the fire, strong enough, tensile as steel, but taking good care not to hurt her. This was the way with them, he realised. No matter the frustrated violence in him, he couldn't bear to hurt her.

He kissed her open mouth that blossomed like a rose, her little moaning breaths gusting back into his. He touched her breast, drew his hand down intimately over her body, bunching the soft denim of her skirt, sliding his hand over a satiny thigh, the length of her leg. The scents of the bush mingled with the scent of her, erotic beyond his understanding. This was how a man and a woman mated, chasing sounds and scents, urgent to know the other's body, as though starved for completion. Two bodies, male and female craving to be one.

"I'm not hurting you," he burst out once, finding her naked breast as delicious as a peach.

"No. I love it." She turned her face into his neck, pressing her lips against his flesh. The damned silly cast on her arm. She was desperate to stroke him as he was stroking her. And yet there was an odd excitement to it, a kind of spice. Gradually, he manoeuvred her clothes away until her body was luminous in the firelight, her blood so heated she felt no chill on her skin. "Ally, are you sure I can't make you pregnant?" he asked urgently, his hand speared into her wonderful hair.

"Make me pregnant," she begged. "Go on, I'd love it."

He stared at her in fascination. "You frighten me. You could lose everything in a minute. Your career."

"No it's an OK time for me," she reassured him. "But I do want your child. Your children. As for my career? Looking back I don't think it existed in the same way it existed for Fee..." She guided his hand down over the smooth curves and planes of her body. "I have something far more important in mind."

He was desperate to believe it. A lie would be fatal. "You can't *do* this, Ally," he said. "I'll never let you go."

She could feel the heat rising from his skin, the male virility, the pounding force of his desire. It was *magnificent*!

"Holding on to your wife is an essential part of marriage," she said with great energy. "How dare you doubt me, Rafe Cameron. I stopped wanting a career long before tonight. I've tried telling you so often, but if you really think about it, you didn't want to hear. In your hurt you made yourself deaf to me."

It bothered him now that there was a good deal of truth in it. "I must have been completely mad."

She nodded in entire agreement. "The bible refers to the sin of pride," she said severely, then she smiled, the wide luminous smile he adored.

"You mean this, Ally? You know your mind?" He pondered her vivid face so full of eloquence.

"How many times do I have to tell you? I'd give my soul for you."

It sent his confidence soaring. Up and up like an eagle in its powerful flight. "And you are the windows of mine."

A feeling of utter exultation seized him, driving out every last lingering doubt. He felt he would conquer the world for her. Rafe cupped her beloved face with his hands, lowering his mouth passionately to hers.

Around them the bush was utterly still and the glittering stars in all their glory crowded down the sky, scattering diamond dust on a pair of lovers.

EPILOGUE

ON THE morning of her wedding day Ally rose early, so full of radiant energy she found she couldn't lie in bed. She dressed in her riding clothes, went quietly through the house filled with wedding guests and out to the stables, saddling up her favourite ride, the beautiful chestnut mare, Aurora, ex-prize-winning racehorse and a present from Brod. Aurora was the ultimate in cooperation or they were perfectly matched, because the mare responded instantly to her lightest instruction.

Twenty minutes later with the dawn wind singing in her ears Ally was galloping across the open grasslands, thrilling to Aurora's speed and power, watching the wonderful glow on the horizon as the sun started into the sky. With the sun came all the glorious rich ochres of the inland. Ever-changing colours that made it such a fascinating place. The pearly grey sky was turning to blue crystal and the birds were out in their millions, every species singing a different melodic line, like instruments in an orchestra, the whole coming together in a perfect, complex, liquidly clear symphony.

Riding was one of her life's greatest pleasures, Ally thought, her mood so buoyant she felt Aurora, like Pegasus might suddenly take wings. She and her horse had developed such a wonderful trusting partnership, a magical harmony. It was far better than driving her BMW but both gave the same feeling of power, of smoothness, of being in control. It was very hard to accept had not some daring Mongolian leapt on a horse's back, the magnificent animal beneath her might have become extinct. Man had to acquire the art of horsemanship before the horse, thought little of eight thousand years ago, was saved from extinction.

She remembered who had taught her to ride as a small child with Brod always a willing helper. It had been Ernie Eaglehawk, Kimbara's finest tracker and horse breaker. The stations owed a big debt to their aboriginal stockmen, the custodians of the ancient land. Ernie had died several years back at a great age but he was one person she would never forget. For his kindness, for the sweetness of his nature, for his natural wisdom. Because of Ernie and his wonderful teaching ability she and Brod were about as good as you get.

She was crossing a shallow home creek when she spotted a rider coming across the plain at a gallop. A moment more and rider and horse took shape. Brod on his majestic Raj. She sat the mare comfortably, waiting for her brother to reach her, saluting him as he reined in alongside.

"Hi, big brother!"

He gave her a brilliant smile. "I told myself that couldn't be Ally. Shouldn't you be in bed resting for your big day?"

"Resting? What are you talking about?" She laughed. "I'm going to enjoy every single minute of it." Her green eyes spilled out radiant light. "Oh, God, I just never knew...."

"I *know.*" Brod continued to smile at her broadly.

"Yes, I know you know. You and Rebecca are so close, so much in love it warms my heart to see it."

Brod's expression grew serious. "She was meant for me as Rafe was meant for you. We didn't have much of an early life, Ally, but it's turning out wonderfully now, isn't it?"

"Dear Brod, I love you," she said. "I love the way you and Rebecca have done everything in your power to make this the most marvellous wedding."

"You deserve it, Ally." Brod gave her a proud smile. "And I love my dual role of giving the bride away and best man. It was the greatest homecoming hearing you and Rafe had resolved all your differences and were finally together again. His joy in you is immense. You know that?"

"He's my man," Ally said, "in every sense of the word. So, we have your blessing?"

Brod gave his white flashing smile. "Ally, so far as I'm concerned you and Rafe marrying is a dream fulfilled." He gathered up the reins, turning the black stallion's head, "What say I race you to the gate of the main compound."

"You're on!" Ally cried. "But don't you dare win!"

"Not on your wedding day," sailed back.

The Outback would long remember the Cameron Kinross wedding, held on historic Kimbara Station, the Kinross flagship. This was the long awaited union of two great pioneering families, and emotions ran high. Guests, three hundred in all, came from every state on the continent, as far away as Texas in the U.S.A. and two of the grand capitals of the world, London and Edinburgh, where both bride and groom had relatives.

As the leading women's magazine reported, the former highly successful TV actress, Ally Kinross, would have four attendants, Lady Francesca de Lyle, her cousin and the only daughter of the internationally famous stage actress Fiona Kinross and Earl of Moray, chief bridesmaid, two of the bride's long-time friends from Sydney, while her sister-in-law Rebecca Kinross, herself not long home from her honeymoon in Europe, would be matron of honour.

The magazine went on to say it had exclusive coverage of the wedding. Their well-known society columnist, Rosemary Roberts, would be in attendance as a guest. The magazine had actually begged to be able to cover one of the biggest weddings of the year. After all, the bride, Alison Kinross, was well-known to the viewing public. The two families were famous in the Outback. The issue would sell like hot cakes. It was later picked up and subsequently reported the substantial sum that changed hands for exclusive coverage, went to one of Mrs. Cameron's favourite causes, the Sydney Children's Hospital.

Her bridesmaids seemed almost spellbound when they saw Ally dressed.

"Well, don't stare at me as though I'm a creature from some mysterious planet," she laughed, so happy her vitality was like a healing ray of sunshine.

"You look...splendid!" Francesca said for all of them, moving around her taking in Ally's magnificent dress. "Like a young queen."

"That's Fee's tiara," Ally suggested, touching it. "Something borrowed. It's perfectly beautiful."

"So are you." Rebecca went to her and gently kissed her cheek, a feather-light touch so as not spoil Ally's flawless make-up. "That was the most wonderful idea featuring the desert wildflowers on your gown. I'm sure it's going to start a rage."

"Could do." Ally nodded in agreement.

She stood still while all her attendants admired her wedding gown of champagne silk-satin and tulle. It was a wedding dress dreams are made of. Strapless with dramatic swathing of a billowing silk-satin skirt leaving a shimmering tulle centre panel embroidered all over with the everlasting daisies of the desert. Thousand upon thousands of tiny beads, rhinestones and crystals had been used to create the small flowers in pinks, white, yellow and gold. The strapless bodice hugged Ally tightly, embroidered tulle moulding the bust, the draped silk satin defining her narrow torso and tiny waist. It was a stunning gown requiring someone tall with a model's figure and posture to wear it. Ally had it all. Her shimmering champagne-coloured tulle veil matched exactly to her dress stood away from Fee's tiara. A necklet of diamonds, Rafe's wedding gift to her, encircled her slender throat. Diamond studs glittered in her ears.

"Now you can all line up for your inspection," Ally said, thrilled with their appearance and the dizzying culmination of her dreams.

"Just a minute!" Francesca rushed to the mirror to adjust her off-the-shoulder neckline from which each sleeve ballooned out. "Ready." Satisfied she joined the line, a titian-haired beauty with shoulders like cream.

Francesca, as chief bridesmaid, wore the pink of the desert wildflower, a glorious contrast with her hair, Jo Anne, a brunette wore the sunshine yellow of the batchelor's buttons, Diane, the blonde, wore the silvery green of the wildflower leaves, Rebecca, as matron of honour, wore gold.

All wore identical styles, the lovely full skirts flaring to the ground. In their hair they wore a crown of real paper daisies with silk leaves, each crown slightly different as were the small matching bouquets. Around each attendant's neck was an 18-carat-gold bezel-set gemstone on a slender gold chain to match their gowns, a pink tourmaline, a yellow sapphire, a peridot and a topaz, a gift from the bridegroom.

"You all look perfectly beautiful." Ally put her hands together in a little burst of applause. "Thank you so much for attending me."

"Oh, Lord, listen to her." Jo Anne laughed. "We're honoured."

"Now you've got something old," Francesca said.

"Yes, dear," Ally nodded. "You've given me that exquisite antique handkerchief."

"Something blue. What about something blue?" Rebecca fluttered around her.

"I'm wearing it." Ally gave a throaty little laugh. "I won't say where."

"Something new?" Diane completed the traditional requirements.

Ally held out her billowing skirt. "It is a brand-new dress." Her smile was incandescent.

"Well, there you are then!" Francesca clutched her hands in delight. "Oh, this is going to be so wonderful. I've got excitement pouring out my ears. I just *love* weddings."

"We'll have to arrange it you're next," Ally told her with a flutter of mischief.

"That's if Mamma doesn't beat me." Francesca only half joked then brightened. "Don't forget I caught part of Rebecca's bouquet, too!"

At exactly three o'clock the ceremony began. Brod guiding his sister through the smiling sea of guests to where the celebrant was waiting on the flower-decked dais of Kimbara's ballroom.

"Be happy, Ally," Brod whispered, feeling a consuming rush of love for her.

Be happy! Ally thought. I'm borne up on wings.

Her hand on her brother's arm, she walked straight to where her bridegroom was standing, straight and tall, his handsome head with the glitter of gold. Now after all these years I'm going to marry the person I've loved all my life!

Rafe and Ally. Mr. and Mrs. Cameron.

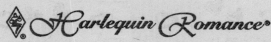

Harlequin Romance®

Are you dreaming of a man who's rich and masterful, foreign and exciting...

Don't miss these thrilling sheikh stories from some of your favorite authors starting in August 2000...

His Desert Rose (#3618)
by Liz Fielding
August 2000

To Marry a Sheikh (#3623)
by Day Leclaire
October 2000

The Sheikh's Bride (#3630)
by Sophie Weston
November 2000

The Sheikh's Reward (#3634)
by Lucy Gordon
December 2000

Enjoy a little Eastern promise...

Available at your favorite retail outlet.

HARLEQUIN®

Makes any time special.™

Back by popular demand are
DEBBIE MACOMBER's

Hard Luck, Alaska, is a town that needs women! And the O'Halloran brothers are just the fellows to fly them in.

Starting in March 2000 this beloved series returns in special 2-in-1 collector's editions:

MAIL-ORDER MARRIAGES, featuring
Brides for Brothers and *The Marriage Risk*
On sale March 2000

FAMILY MEN, featuring
Daddy's Little Helper and *Because of the Baby*
On sale July 2000

THE LAST TWO BACHELORS, featuring
Falling for Him and *Ending in Marriage*
On sale August 2000

Collect and enjoy each MIDNIGHT SONS story!

Available at your favorite retail outlet.

HARLEQUIN®
Makes any time special ™